GOL...

By Lawrence De Maria
Copyright © Lawrence De Maria 2019

Published by St. Austin's Press (305-409-0900)

Dedicated to my wife, *Patricia*, without whose love,

support and faith this book

— and others —

would not have been possible,

and to my sons,

Lawrence and Christopher.

Good men, both.

CHAPTER 1 - FRAGRANT
San Francisco

The two men were an all-too-common sight in San Francisco, even in the toniest of neighborhoods.

Hundreds of derelicts, vagrants, homeless — however they were labeled — slept on the streets. Or, rather, in doorways, behind bushes, on porches, in backyards and alleys. Raggedly-dressed and almost always fragrant, the "street people" had found an oasis in this, the most-liberal big city in America, even if they had long since worn out their welcome among many citizens.

Because rents and selling prices in San Francisco was so absurdly high — certain neighborhoods made Manhattan look inexpensive — residents could not argue that the homeless were hurting property values. It didn't matter if a homeless person was eating, sleeping, and occasionally defecating in the yard of a duplex when each of its two apartments had a waiting list of people willing to pay $5,000 a month in rent.

Of course, after enough complaints, "fragrant vagrants" as they were called, could be rousted by the police and moved on. Only to be replaced by other poor souls. Many of the street people were veterans, ignored by a country awash in on-the-sleeve patriotism but short on real sympathy.

One could argue that San Francisco at least had a heart, if not common sense.

But the duo huddling on cardboard boxes in a doorway next to the Calypso Towers on Drumm Street were not homeless. They had a nice apartment in Noe

Valley and were gainfully employed, even if that employment was criminal.

"You smell like a dead yak," the much taller of the two men told his companion.

"Smotrite kto zagovoril," the other man replied.

"I know I do," the man replied, laughing. "But speak English! Do you want to attract attention?"

"It doesn't matter," the man said, but this time in heavily accented English. "No one will come near us smelling like this. I can hardly keep from puking. Give me a cigarette."

Both men had smeared their pants cuffs with dog feces, also in good supply on the streets of San Francisco. They had not shaved in a week, nor washed their hair. Their jackets, cargo pants, socks and boots had been purchased in an Army-Navy store and manually caked with dirt and mud.

They wanted to wear clean underwear, but their boss was afraid they might wind up in the morgue, hospital or jail. Even without identification, clean underwear would arouse suspicion.

So, they went "commando." A real inconvenience in the city, which got cold many nights, especially this close to the waterfront. They had cased their target for a week, timing his comings and goings. They had become fixtures in the neighborhood, ignored and tolerated.

Yes, they were often cold and uncomfortable, but they had suffered the same indignities, only worse, in other climates.

***

"Come on, wake up," the taller man said. "It's

time."

The night was dark and misty. Perfect. No one was about and everyone in the apartment building was presumably asleep, except the guard at the desk in the lobby. He was the building's only nighttime security, and was just one member of a small maintenance staff that rotated the desk job. Unlike newer apartment complexes, Calypso Towers had no security cameras, although the building's management company had suggested they be installed. The condo board that handled such matters had scheduled a vote on buying such cameras for the next month's meeting.

"What time is it?" his partner said, drowsily.

"Just after 4."

Slipping into the apartment building unseen at 4 A.M. was a cinch, especially for men of their experience. Through a bush, over a short wall to an unguarded rear door. It was a lot safer than going in the front door, where the lobby guard would certainly stop two smelly vagrants from getting past him. And killing the guard was out of the question. That would negate all their hard work.

The rear entrance was locked, accessible only if someone had a key card. Just like the one they had, compliments of their employer, who had rented an apartment in the same building under an assumed name just for this eventuality.

Once inside, the men took the stairs. They were breathing heavily once they reached the floor on which their target lived. Cautiously opening the stairwell door, they looked in both directions down the corridor. They were alone.

The door to the apartment was also locked. The lock was easy pickings. The apartment was dark and the men moved silently, using only the light from a cell phone to guide them. They had been given a schematic of the one-bedroom apartment but they cautiously paused every few feet and listened. The only thing they heard was the faint sound of snoring. As they crept, the shorter "vagrant" took a small bottle and a handkerchief from his pocket.

Except for his snoring, their victim was sleeping soundly, on top of the sheets in his underclothes. The man with the bottle sprinkled a few drops of liquid on the handkerchief, careful not to breathe the fumes. The sleeping man was on his back, making it easy to cover his mouth with the chloroformed material. His eyes popped open, but after a brief struggle he was out again.

"Stay with him," his partner said. "I'll see to his computer."

"How come you get to write the note?"

"My English is better."

"How am I supposed to learn?"

"Not on the job, you dunce! Otherwise we will both be taking language class in prison. Now, just make sure he stays asleep."

"Don't forget to open the sliders. It will be easier later."

Ten minutes later, the taller man came back to the bedroom.

"Let's get him dressed," he said.

That was part of the plan. It was hard work putting a suit, tie, socks and shoes on an unconscious man.

"He's coming to," the shorter man said. "Should I give him another few drops."

"Forget it. He's ready to go. Let's get this over with."

They dragged the man out. At the last minute he came awake.

It was too late.

***

Joyce Lockhart always liked to be the first person in the pool in the morning, even if it was at 7:15 on a typically chilly Wednesday morning in October.

Chilly? It was freezing, she thought as she shed her terrycloth robe and headed to the low diving board in the deep end of the outdoor pool in the rear of the 12-story apartment building. She dropped the robe and her key card on a lounge chair.

She was wearing a rather old-fashioned one-piece black bathing suit and a white bathing cap. The suit was too tight, and bulged a bit at her midriff. But, as she had hoped, she was alone. And while that pleased her, she did feel a bit uneasy.

The pool was a "dawn-to-dusk" facility, and even when it was busier later in the day, there was no lifeguard. "SWIM AT YOUR OWN RISK" signs, along with a long list of rules (no babies or incontinent seniors without diapers, no open wounds, etc.), were prominently posted near the life preservers and long rescue poles hanging on the chain-link fence along both sides of the pool. Seeing the health warnings, she often wondered what public swimming was like in San Francisco during the height of the A.I.D.S epidemic, when those horrible lesions were so prevalent.

Having other people at the pool meant that someone would be able to dive in or at least use the emergency equipment. So, June Lockhart swam before she ate anything, even though she knew that the 30-minute rule had recently been debunked. And, of course, barring a heart attack, seizure or brain aneurysm, as a strong swimmer she knew she could easily reach the side of the pool.

It was Joyce's belief that gradually entering cold water anywhere, be it pool, lake or ocean, only increased the torture. She had lived in San Francisco for only a few years, but learned her lesson the first time she went swimming in the Pacific Ocean in the summer. Brought up in New Jersey, she assumed that the water in August, especially after a recent heat wave, would be warm, as it was invariably along the Jersey shore.

She was soon disabused of that notion.

The Pacific is many times larger than the Atlantic, and always cold, even down in Los Angeles. And at San Francisco's latitude, it is even colder. Her first dip at China Beach was an eye opener. Even though it was a protected lagoon not directly fronting the Pacific, the water was shockingly frigid. After that experience, June just dove right in, the initial shock much better than incremental submersion.

As for her building's pool, she always headed for the lower of the two diving boards at the deep end. Fall temperatures at night rarely got above 60 degrees, and while the pool had a heat pump that was supposed to store warmth overnight, it only made the water bearable. And sometimes the pump was broken, as she found out one tooth-jarring morning!

It was only when June walked out to the end of her board and bounced up and down a few times, working up the courage to dive in, that she glanced over and noticed that there was no high diving board jutting out from its platform.

Joyce shrugged.

They were always repairing something at Calypso Towers. Or maybe it was a safety issue. A few of the residents had complained that, despite warning signs about tampering with the tension wheels that controlled the bounce of the diving boards, some of the teens did anyway. The boys adjusted the high-dive board so that they could spring higher and farther, often cartwheeling loudly through the air like lunatics, usually to impress some girls. Sooner or later, one of the idiots would hit the side of the pool or dive too deeply and wind up a paraplegic.

Perhaps fearing a lawsuit in litigious California, the building's directors had probably decided to eliminate the high board.

Joyce Lockhart assumed she missed the notice on the lobby bulletin board. She jounced on her board a few feet above the water. She was a low-board gal, anyway. And her age, 43, and a tad overweight (15 pounds and that is coming off!) she believed that going off a high board was a bit unseemly.

Joyce looked down and prepared to plunge in. With no one around, she briefly contemplated a cannonball. Very briefly. Talk about unseemly.

A slight patchy mist hovered over the pool water. She put her hands above her head and bent her knees.

Suddenly, she stopped. There was something bobbing in the water just below her. It took her a moment to realize what it was. It was the top of a long board, floating vertically, most of its length shimmering below the surface.

It was the missing high board.

That was odd. What the hell was it doing in the pool? It was an obvious danger. Motivated by the current generated by the pool's filter pumps, the board floated closer to the side of the pool.

Joyce Lockhart dove in. The shock of hitting the cool water wasn't as bad as she expected, probably because she had something else on her mind. Mainly, the high-diving board, which Joyce planned to remove from the pool, or, if it proved too cumbersome, to at least secure it a safe distance from the board area.

But the next shock was exponentially greater.

As she reached the nadir of her dive and opened her eyes prior to arching to the surface, Joyce Lockhart came face to face with a man lying on his back at the bottom of the pool. His eyes were open, and trickles of blood seeped from his broken and flattened nose, and both ears. His arms were outstretched and seemed to be beckoning her.

Her first instinct was to scream. A mistake. She took in some water. Broaching the surface, she coughed and sputtered to the side of the pool.

Joyce didn't know what to do. She suppressed an urge to vomit and then thought about diving back down to help the man but dismissed the idea immediately. He was so obviously dead.

So, it was back to her first instinct.

Joyce Lockhart screamed.

CHAPTER 2 - DEAD POOL

"His name is Allenby, Detective. I think. Something like that."

Charles Lin, annoyed, looked up from the body, which was now lying at the side of the pool, with rivulets of water draining from its sodden clothes.

The cops in the responding area car had pulled the body from the water only a few minutes earlier, just before Lin showed up. The water near the torso's head was tinged pink. Someone had placed a towel across the man's face. Lin had pulled it back. He wondered if it had been one of the spectators or one of the first cops on the scene. If it was a cop, that was a breach of crime-scene protocol. Bodies were to be left the way they were found until a detective or medical examiner finished with them.

He could ask, but what was the point? Either way, whoever used the towel probably thought he or she was doing the decent thing, since the dead man's visage was not pleasant to look at. Finding out what caused the facial damage would be the first order of business.

Lin shrugged and replaced the towel. No harm, no foul. He had been squatting but now stood up.

"It's Inspector, sir," he said, facing the man who had spoken up. "And you are?"

"Name is Dieter. Felix Dieter. Aren't you a detective?"

The man appeared to be at least 80. Very thin, with scraggly white hair, unshaven, liver spots galore and dressed like he just threw on the first things he saw.

Black sweater with several holes, checkered-red shirt, brown-striped shorts and polka-dot socks shoved into slippers. Although, Lin ruminated, the old guy probably always dressed like that.

"You ain't wearing a uniform like those guys."

Dieter pointed to a group of blue-uniformed patrol officers from the San Francisco Police Department, some of whom were walking the perimeter and some of whom were keeping the curious at a distance.

"In this city, we are called Inspector, sir," Lin said.

"Well, whoopie doo. Didn't know that. Like those investigators on those BBC police shows. *Midsomer Murders*, right, Inspector Sir!"

The man actually saluted.

"No! Just Inspector."

"Whatever. Anyway, I live on the second floor. I came out on my terrace when I heard the woman. I was fixin' a cup of coffee. Damn near dropped the cup. That gal can scream, I tell you. Got some set of lungs. And I don't mean her titties, which are nothing to write home about from the looks of them in her bathing suit. Not that I blame her for losing it. Looked down and saw her sprawled by the side of the pool. Figured she was having a fit or something and I came out to get her away from the pool, in case she fell in, you know. Lucky I was already dressed."

Lin suppressed a smile.

"You tell all this to the uniformed officer over there?"

Lin pointed to a cop who was taking statements from the growing scrum of people standing at the shallow end of the pool.

"Yup. He's a nice young fellow."

The way Dieter said it made it obvious that he didn't think Lin was all that nice.

"And he told you to stay where you were, right?"

The man furrowed his brow.

"Well, no. But I figured you'd want an identification."

"The man is dressed," Lin said. "He might have a wallet."

"Did he?"

"No," Lin admitted, having already checked the man's pockets.

"There you go," Dieter said, smugly.

Inspector Lin sighed. He had just been clearing up some paperwork in Central Station before heading home after an overnight shift when he got the call about the body. Another ten minutes and someone else would have caught it.

The S.F.P.D. covers ten districts, with a station in each. Central covered the Financial District, Chinatown, North Beach, Fisherman's Wharf, and the iconic Telegraph, Nob and Russian Hills. Being an Inspector in Central, as Lin was, is considered a plum assignment. Most days.

This wasn't shaping up to be one of those days, Lin thought. He loved his job but wanted to go home to get some sleep. Leslie would have gotten the kids off and would know better than to want sex after Lin got off the night tour. Although with the kids in school, you never knew about Leslie.

"Looks to me like a suicide," Felix Dieter opined.

Lin ignored the remark. The body was found

almost fully dressed in the pool of an exclusive high-rise building. Until the Medical Examiner said otherwise, Lin would treat the situation as a potential homicide.

"Allenby, that was his name? You're sure?"

"Pretty sure. Something like that."

"First name?"

"Don't know it. Only seen him in the elevator a couple of times. We're kinda new to the building. I get off on the second floor. He keeps going up."

The old man chuckled.

"Except this time, you'd have to say. He went down."

He saw the look on the cop's face.

"Not funny, I guess. Sorry."

Lin sighed. He was in no mood for humor, in poor taste or not.

"That's a hell of an I.D., sir. His name may or may not be Allenby and he lives on a floor above you. Unless he was just visiting someone, of course."

Dieter looked at Lin. He wondered if all Chinese detectives, or inspectors, whatever the hell they were called, were so snippy.

"No, sonny. He lived here. Spoke to him once or twice. Just to say hello. He was carrying groceries and mail."

Dieter turned away and yelled.

"Hey, Phyllis, that guy we met last week on the elevator. Name is Allenby, right."

Phyllis used a walker and started to head over to the body. A uniformed cop tried to stop her.

"That's my wife," Dieter said. "She'll know. Only

14

been here a year and already she knows everything about anything in the building."

He rolled his eyes.

"Just ask her, *In-spec-tor*. She'll tell you."

Lin, sounding defeated, told the cop to let the woman through. When she finally reached the side of the pool and the body, she looked scornfully at her husband.

"Don't listen to my husband. His name was Allender. *A-l-l-e-n-d-e-r*. Lived on the top floor. Was a broker. Lived alone. Quiet. Did he jump?"

"What makes you think that?"

Now, Phyllis Dieter rolled her eyes.

"Because he lived right up there, like I said, on the 12th floor. Directly above the pool. Didn't think he'd go swimming fully dressed, now, do you? It's the quiet ones you got to worry about. If they're not serial killers, they're suicidal. A lot of brokers jump out of windows during financial crashes, don't they."

"There's no crash now," her husband interjected. He looked at his wife. "I watch the financial news on FOX. I would have heard about it."

"Maybe he knew something we don't know about yet," his wife said. "That's why he jumped. Knew the markets were about to go into the crapper. I think we should check our retirement portfolio."

She looked at the police officer.

"We're on a fixed income, you know. And the rent here eats most of it up. I told Felix we should have stayed in Ohio. But no, he had his heart set on San Francisco. Like Tony Bennett or something."

"Tony Bennett sang with Lady Gaga," Felix Dieter

said, as if that meant something.

Lin's head was spinning. Ten more goddamn minutes and he would have been spared this.

"Ma'am, how did you know he was a broker?"

"He told me he worked in the financial district, just down the street."

"Doesn't mean he was a broker."

"What else would he be, jumping off his deck."

It was obvious that the old lady thought her logic was irrefutable.

"Don't matter, anyway," her husband said. "He's dead, isn't he?"

Phyllis Dieter looked down at the corpse's feet, which were unshod. The man's socks, dark blue with little yellow horses on them, were bundled around his ankles.

"You can tell he wasn't married or had a live-in lady," Phyllis Dieter said.

Lin stared at her.

"One of his socks is on inside-out," she explained. "I wouldn't let Felix out of the house with socks inside-out."

Then she cracked a small smile.

"Besides, I asked around. Like to know about my neighbors. One can't be too careful nowadays."

She glanced at the corpse.

"Where's his shoes?"

"They were at the bottom of the pool," Lin said.

"Loafers, right?"

Lin nodded.

"Probably came off when he hit the water," she said, "or the board. Must have hit it. Felix said his face was all mashed."

"I didn't say it was all mashed. His nose is flattened like a pancake, but it's him for sure."

"You said something about a board, Mrs. Dieter?" Lin asked.

The old woman sighed.

"The diving board, sonny. That one, floating over there. Probably find all sorts of DNA on it. Don't you watch N.C.I.S.?"

Lin hated TV cop shows, where all it took to solve a crime was a computer and a smart phone.

He looked up. And then back down to the pool area. The high-diving platform ended abruptly. No board.

He tilted his head. The angle looked about right. The forensic guys would have to check it out, but the old crone was probably correct.

"I thought I heard a big splash last night," Felix Dieter said.

CHAPTER 3 - BLADDER

Lin stared at him.

"I just remembered, sonny," Dieter said.

The Inspector suppressed a cutting remark. The man was, after all, old. Lin, while thoroughly American, had a respect for elders ingrained by his Chinese heritage.

"What time was that, sir?"

"Oh, I don't know. Probably 3 or 4 a.m. I had just gone to the bathroom."

"Prostate," his wife explained. "He pees 10 times a night."

"It's not that often, Phyllis."

"Seems like it."

Felix Dieter looked embarrassed.

"My prostate is the size of Iowa, Inspector. But, honest, I go only five or six times a night. Anyways, I heard a splash, but I thought it was some of the kids that live in the building. They are always horsing around in the pool."

Lin again looked up.

"Which is your apartment, sir?'

Dieter pointed to the second floor.

"Right there."

"The slider is closed."

"Wasn't last night. At least not all the way. I leave it open a crack. Sometimes I fall asleep on the recliner. I like the fresh air. At night I can smell the ocean."

"He's left it open when it rains," his wife said, accusingly. "I keep telling him not to."

Lin thought no one would blame Felix Dieter if he

jumped one day. Of course, it was only two stories.

"That's it, a splash, sir? Nothing else?"

"Might have heard a scream."

"Might have?"

"Kids are always screaming, yelling, you know. Gave it the same notice I gave the splash."

"I had the TV on in the den," Phyllis Dieter interjected. "I sleep on the couch in there, rather than listen to Felix get up every hour to urinate. Maybe he heard a scream from the TV."

Lin turned to the man.

"Could that have been what you heard?"

Felix Dieter considered it.

"I guess. But it was kind of long."

"Long?"

"You know, drawn out. I don't think it was from the TV."

Lin thought that over.

"You heard the woman who found the body scream. And that made you look out. Why didn't you look out when you heard the first scream?"

"Never heard no scream like hers. Could have woke the dead."

"Not all of them," Lin said under his breath.

"What did you say?"

"Nothing, sir. They let people swim in the dark here?"

"Kids are kids," the man said. "Not supposed to go in the pool after dusk. That's what the sign says. Must be damned cold. But kids are kids. I did some crazy things when I was young, too."

"Bet you didn't pee 10 times a night," his wife

huffed.

She looked at the Inspector.

"When he was a young man, he could knock over ten pins. Lousy aim, though. I was always cleaning up the toilet."

I need a drink, Lin thought. Even if it's only just after 9 a.m.

One of the uniforms walked over.

"Forensics is here, Inspector."

Lin looked over and saw three men draped in baggy white overalls and holding rectangular black cases. One of them waved to him.

"They'll have to drain the pool," Lin said. "Also, I want them to check that board."

He pointed at the diving board, which was still in the pool.

"And the high-dive platform. The vic might have hit the high board on the way down."

"Ouch," the cop said.

"Ouch, indeed. Any word on the M.E.?"

"On the way. He was in Ingleside. Stuck in traffic on the 280."

Lin knew that the Ingleside Station was all the way across town. It might be a while in rush hour. His stomach rumbled.

"OK. Thanks."

The uniform walked away.

"Aren't you supposed to leave the body where you find it until the medical examiner looks at it," Felix Dieter said, trying to regain the high ground. He watched N.C.I.S., too.

"Oh boy, that's rich," his wife hooted. "Maybe the

M.E. would have put on scuba gear like Lloyd Bridges in *Sea Hunt* and do an underwater autopsy."

"He went through the man's pockets, too," Felix Dieter said, defensively.

"Probably looking for identification," his wife said, dismissively. "Sometimes they do that on N.C.I.S., too."

She looked at Lin.

"Right, Inspector?"

"Yes, ma'am," he said, wondering just who was running the investigation.

"You ever watch *Sea Hunt*? Nah. You're too young. Before your time. But you should watch N.C.I.S."

She paused for effect.

"Pick up a few pointers. You carrying a knife?"

"A knife?"

"Jethro says you should never go anywhere without a knife."

"Jethro?"

"The N.C.I.S. special agent Mark Harmon plays," the old woman said, obviously exasperated by Lin's ignorance. "He's in charge. It's his Rule 9."

If I had a knife, Lin thought, I'd probably cut my own throat right about now. He took a deep breath.

"I will start watching, ma'am. Soon as I get home tonight."

"Not tonight," she said. "The show is on Tuesdays. Of course, they have reruns just about every night, on cable. So, you can catch up. I think the old ones are the best, with Tony and Ziva."

"Can't wait. Now, you said Mr. Allender lived on

the 12th floor. Would you happen to know what apartment he occupied?"

"Well, we're in 206," Felix Dieter said, glad to have some input. "And if he hit the board like she said, he'd be in 1206. Board is right below our place. Apartments are numbered the same on every floor."

"If it was me," Phyllis Dieter said. "I'd have gone up to the roof. Give myself another 10 or 20 feet, just to make sure."

"Maybe he was superstitious," Felix said, and cackled.

The other two looked at him.

"You know, the roof would have been the 13th floor. Jumping off of it would have been bad luck."

The old man laughed some more.

"You're sick," his wife said.

Actually, Lin thought, now that I get it, it wasn't a bad line. Maybe the old codger still has a few moves left.

"Anyway, I sure wouldn't have jumped anywhere near the pool," his wife said. "Some people can survive hitting the water. Even jumpers off the Golden Gate sometimes live. Of course, they have safety nets there now."

"I don't think another few feet would have made any difference," Felix said. "Besides, it's a pain in the butt to get up on the roof. They usually keep it locked. Poor fellow. Just think, Phyllis, he musta gone right by our window."

"Lucky you didn't see that," she said, "or you would have peed 11 times."

Lin glanced quickly down at the body. I wish to

hell I knew for sure whether you screamed on the way down.

Suicides usually don't. Unless they have second thoughts on the way down. Lin looked up to the 12th floor. Allender wouldn't have had much time for second thoughts.

By the time he reconsidered, he'd have been dead.

CHAPTER 4 - ABBY
New York City

The pigeon on the windowsill cocked his head at me. Or maybe it was *her* head. Pigeons aren't pheasants, so it's hard to tell.

Whatever its sex, the bird stared at me. Curiosity? Do birds think? I knew the pejorative term "birdbrain" is unfair to our feathered friends. Given its size relative to body weight, a bird's brain is not insignificant. Apparently, some crows and parrots can add and subtract, which is more than many kids in today's public schools.

Since it is widely accepted that modern birds are genetically descended from dinosaurs, it made me wonder where the dinosaurs were headed before that big comet obliterated them and about 90 percent of all above-ground life 60 million years ago. Prior to that ecological catastrophe, early mammals were small and lived mostly underground in holes, mainly so that they would not become toe jam when stepped on by some T-Rex or brontosaurus. Without that comet, dinosaurs might have eventually ruled the Earth intellectually.

Given current events, I'm not sure that comet did Earth any favors, evolution-wise.

Maybe my pigeon was staring at me and thinking about how dumb I was sitting at my desk, inside, breathing stale air, on such a nice day. And, as if to prove the point, it flew away.

Hah! You can't do that human brain! Well, what can I expect from a creature that evolved from a frightened little mole!

"What the hell are you talking about, boss?"

I came out of my avian reverie, brought my feet down and swiveled my desk chair to face Abby, who had just walked into my office. I realized that I had been talking aloud as I imagined my pigeon's thoughts.

"Did you know birds are very smart," I said. "And that they are descended from the dinosaurs."

She gave me the Abby look, perfected over the years. It wasn't the first time she caught me, feet on my desk, staring out my window

"Things are a bit slow here, huh boss?"

That was certainly true. My bank account was still solid, but I had more time on my hands than I liked.

"Have they found Amelia Earhart yet? I'm thinking about giving it a shot."

She laughed.

"So, boss, is this the weekend?"

Habika (Abby) Jones smiled. She is a happy person and smiles easily. But this one had a Cheshire-cat undercurrent. Something was up.

"Abs, you don't have to call me boss," I said. "You don't work for me anymore. You have your own office. For Crissakes, you even have a secretary, which I don't have. Anymore."

"Leslie is not my secretary. He is my assistant, which is what I was when I worked here."

"Actually, your last title was "office manager"."

Abby was now sitting in a client chair across from me, having just poured us two mugs of coffee from the pot I had warming in its Mr. Coffee carafe sitting atop the small fridge in the corner.

"Jill of all trades was more like it," she said. "How do you like my new outfit?"

It was a minefield question. Abby was not a small woman. Sturdy was a word that came to mind, although I'd never use it to her face. She was wearing a maroon turtleneck sweater, under a dark-blue jacket. Her trousers were gray. I had to admit, everything seemed to fit nicely. So nicely that I took a chance.

"You look great, Abs. Have you lost weight?"

There was a long pause, during which I contemplated following the pigeon off the ledge.

"Well, it's about damn time you noticed. Some detective you are. I'm down ten pounds. Been working out like a bastard."

Whew!

Abby took a sip of coffee and winced.

"And I made a better pot of coffee when I worked here. That machine is idiot-proof. How did you screw this up? Tastes like precinct coffee."

The ultimate insult. For some reason I felt compelled to defend my coffee-making expertise.

"Kalugin likes it," I said, lamely.

"Maks would drink battery acid," Abby said.

Maks Kalugin was the fearsome bodyguard and occasional assassin who protected Arman Rahm, a high-school acquaintance of mine who took over what was once a totally criminal Russian family on Staten Island. The Rahms once debated killing me, but that aside, we've become fairly good friends, especially as Arman developed more legitimate outlets for the family.

"I bet Rahm won't drink this swill," Abby added.

She was right. During his occasional visits, Arman Rahm, who was always a bit of a dandy, brought his own coffee. I sighed.

"Guy in the supermarket talked me into a new blend," I said. "Turns out it is coarse-ground and appropriate for a French Press, not a Mr. Coffee."

"French Press. That's the one you pour in hot water, stir, wait for it to reach the right whatever and then press the plunger?"

I nodded.

"Seems like a lot of work."

"Which is why I don't have one," I said.

Although Arman has been trying to talk me into buying one. And a samovar, for good measure.

"You have your office up and running, Abs?"

"Yeah. Omar just left. Got me set up so I can probably hack the Russians hacking us."

Omar was one of Abby's brothers and worked for the cable company.

"How is Leslie working out?"

"Pretty good, so far. Considering that when I got his résumé I thought he was she."

"Leslie can go either way, name wise. Leslie Howard was a big Hollywood heartthrob in the 1930's. Played Ashley Wilkes in *Gone With the Wind*. Nazis killed him when he went back to Europe."

"He was a Jew?"

"No. Just in the wrong place, or wrong plane, at the time. They shot down his airliner."

"A real gone with the wind, huh? My Leslie can go both ways, more than name-wise. Mostly men, though."

That didn't bother me, but I hadn't known that. I'd met Leslie once or twice, and he'd seemed straight. I remembered being in the elevator with him once when a couple of young women flirted with him. I also remembered being annoyed because they ignored me. For some reason Tab Hunter and Rock Hudson popped into my head.

"Abby, you have to be the only black private eye in the city with a gay white guy as an assistant. I hope you never have to fire him. Instant discrimination suit."

She laughed.

"He's handicapped, too!"

"You're joking. He seemed OK to me."

"Has a prosthetic leg."

"You'd never know it. He doesn't even limp."

"Is that a gay slur?"

We both laughed.

"A modern prosthesis is amazing. Leslie lost his left leg below the knee in Afghanistan. He was an Army Ranger."

"Good Lord! A handicapped war veteran, too! He checks off all the boxes."

"You were wounded in Afghanistan, too, weren't you?'

"Yeah. And before me, Maks, when the Russians were cocking it up. People have been fighting in that godforsaken place forever. I think the first casualty was a Neanderthal."

"Just like the folks who run the wars now," Abby said. "Anyway, I just had to hire Leslie. I doubt anything will surprise him. I don't know how long he will be with me. He just wanted a steady gig for a couple of years to help pay for his degree at Wagner. Your pal, Clapper, helped him get some scholarship dough."

Dave Clapper formerly headed the Coast Guard base on Staten Island. After retiring from the Coasties, he became Chief of Staff to the Wagner College president, Spencer Bradley. He never hesitates to help out a veteran. I vaguely recalled Abby asking me if she could use my name if she had to call Clapper. I guess she did.

"Well, if push comes to shove, the boys upstairs will probably take your case, pro bono."

Abby's mobile phone buzzed.

"I gotta take this," she said, and went into my now-vacant outer office.

CHAPTER 5 - TRIGGER

While I waited for Abby to return, I took my coffee over to the window and looked out at New York Harbor.

The day was clear and cold. In the distance two Staten Island ferries were passing each other in opposite directions. That reminded me and I looked at my watch. I still had plenty of time. Alice said she was catching the 4:20 from Manhattan. I knew she would be cutting it close after the 1 PM class she taught on Fridays. She'd call if there was a problem.

Tankers, freighters and huge container ships plied the Narrows, some herded by big Moran tugs. Off to my right, the Verrazzano Bridge arched proudly to Brooklyn, probably because it was now spelled correctly. For 50 years the signage in and around the span had been missing the second "z" in Verrazzano, which was how Giovanni de Verrazzano, the bridge's 15th-Century Italian explorer namesake, spelled his moniker. The error was caused by a typo in the original construction contact.

One wonders what else slipped through in the contract. Giovanni certainly didn't care now, but a Jewish state senator with a lot of Italian constituents in Brooklyn did, and $4 million was allocated to fix the 100 or so signs. Some wags wondered why there never seemed to be enough money to fix potholes, but considering that the bridge has been paid off for decades and tolls continue to rise I thought quibbling over a few million bucks wasted on a bunch of "z's" missed the big picture.

In the distance, to my left, the Freedom Tower dominated the lower tip of Manhattan. But not like its predecessors used to dominate it. I was having a hard time warming up to their replacement. I knew the new tower was architecturally more pleasing and allegedly sounder (sure), but I missed the Twin Towers.

Only one office in my building, on the top floor just above me, had a better view. That office occupied the entire ninth floor and was owned, as was the building, by a law firm. Abby's office was on the second floor. It was smaller and had no view. But it was free, which is an even better deal than the below-market rent I was paying.

Abby and I have a symbiotic relationship with the once all-male law firm, which, of course, now also has women associates. When I was getting back on my professional feet after my Army Reserve call-up and subsequent injuries, the lawyers, some of whom I knew from high school, threw me a lot of skip trace and insurance grunt work, which I did for free in return for a substantial rent break in what was then a half-vacant building.

But even when the real estate market firmed, they kept my rent low. That may have had something to do with some high-price referrals I sent them, including an endless environmental lawsuit against a Fortune 500 corporation that stored radioactive material in what is now a residential neighborhood full of kids.

Abby was the researcher who helped put together that case, so they love her. I'm not rich, but I've become a "go-to" guy in the business, so I've told the law firm to throw the skip and insurance work Abby's way. As they know, she is a whiz at computers and research. She once located a guy who hadn't even moved into his new house in Toledo. A process server greeted the poor schmuck as he carried his luggage to the front door. I heard that the server even helped the man with his bags.

I'd met Abby when she was a security guard behind the desk in the lobby. We hit it off almost immediately, our friendship sealed by a mutual love of eggplant parmigiana hero sandwiches from the nearby Red Lantern tavern, which I supplied to her liberally. Omar the cable brother treated me like family and is basically on call whenever I have a problem. That makes me the envy of all the other tenants in the office building. I don't feel sorry for them. They could have bought the subs, too. Looking at Abby now, I suspected she'd cut back on the eggplant.

Another of Abby's brothers, Leon, has morphed from a frequently incarcerated gang banger into respected gangster with political connections and powerhouse attorneys. I believe that in the current political environment he has an outside chance to become President.

If anything, Leon is more important to me. While Omar has saved my internet life, Leon has saved my actual life.

As a retired Army M.P., Abby's knowledge of crime and forensics made her too valuable to be sitting behind a security desk, and I eventually offered her a job. She's proved her worth many times over, never more so than a case when she convinced the cops that a hanging "suicide" was a murder. The length of rope and the victim's drop were too short to account for the broken neck the Medical Examiner listed as the cause of death.

With my help, it didn't take her long to get her P.I. license and set up her own shop. Staten Island's demographics are changing. Once a heavily all-white, sparsely populated bastion in the heart of one of biggest megalopolises on the planet, the borough is now home to almost half a million people, many of them minorities. As the island's only female private eye, of any color, she will do well.

Abby came back and filled our cups before sitting down. Coffee is coffee. I came away from the window and also sat. I didn't ask her about the call. She'd tell me if she wanted me to know about it.

"Where were we? Oh yes, I asked you a question. Is this the weekend?"

The smile was back.

"What do you mean?"

"That you make an honest woman out of Alice?"

"Alice may be the most honest woman I've ever met."

"You know what I mean, Alton Rhode."

"What happened to boss?"

"What happened to answering my question? I know she's coming to the Island for the weekend. When are you going to ask the girl to marry you?"

"What are you, a black yenta?"

"If you mean matchmaker, the proper Yiddish term is 'shadchanit'," Abby said. "Yenta means aristocratic, or noble. Of course, that might apply to me, too."

I stared at her.

"Cormac explained the difference," she added.

"When did you speak to him?"

"Couple of days ago. Wanted to see how he was doing."

Cormac Levine was still recovering from being shot in his doorway, an incident that prompted both his retirement from the Police Department and a move to New Jersey.

"And you discussed Yiddish phraseology?"

"We discussed you and Alice, and the terms came up. He and Irene think like I do."

Jesus, a conspiracy.

"What makes you all think I want to get married? Or that Alice does?"

"I know she wants to. And you do to, even if you don't know it."

"Just how do you know?"

"I am descended from African witchdoctors. I have a powerful instinct about things of the heart."

"So, you want to rain on my parade?"

"Very funny. You are thinking about Indian witchdoctors."

"The proper term is Native-American witchdoctors. What kind of oppressed minority are you? Besides, I think you are busting my balls. Witchdoctors, indeed."

Abby laughed, got up and headed back to her office. At my door she turned.

"I made that witchdoctor crap up. But I'm serious about the rest. Everyone knows you two are made for each other. One of you has to pull the trigger, and while I know it's a brave new world, I still think that's a man's job."

CHAPTER 6 - BLUE BOX

Of course, Abby was right. I'd been kicking the idea around in my head for weeks, though I'd never admit it to anyone, least of all Abby.

I'd met Alice at the Wagner College pool some years earlier. I was rehabbing some minor war wounds and she was doing double duty teaching philosophy and coaching the women's swim team. She noticed my bullet holes. I noticed her legs.

After a rough start that included running her then boyfriend, a felonious professor, out of town, we fell in love. She now is tenured at Barnard in Manhattan and lives in an apartment in Greenwich Village. We live separate but monogamous lives, spending a lot of time together in each other's homes.

It's only recently that I've been getting vibes that Alice wanted to make our arrangement more formal.

Alice was married, once, very young. The union was brief, and she's barely talked about it.

I've never been married. And while I have nothing against the institution, I've also never really thought about it, until recently, and realized the obvious: Alice was, indeed, the one. I mean, how many brilliant, beautiful and sexually bountiful women am I going to fall in love with? Who would love a lug like me?

I looked at my watch again. It was time to pick her up. I went over to the wall in my office where I'd hung a print of a wooden sailing vessel under construction in what was once called Linoleumville and is now the community of Travis. The print, by a famous local artist named John Noble, was a recent gift from Alice.

I took the frame off the wall and put it on my desk. Then I entered a code in the keypad of another recent gift, one I made to myself, of a small safe that fit snugly between two wall studs. I took out a small dark-blue box, closed the safe and returned the print.

I opened the box. A&B Jewelers on New Dorp Lane had done a fine re-setting of the diamond my mother had passed on to me from her mother. The center stone in the new setting is only two carats, but is surrounded by six smaller diamonds. I wasn't pinching pennies, but the additional gemstones had cost me a lot less than I thought they would.

I smiled to myself and thought about the time my neighbor, Al Johnsen, had gotten a poison-pen letter accusing him of having an unkempt yard. Al was enraged by two things. First off, other men on our block in other letters had been accused of various sexcapades, and Al thought his manhood was being impugned. Secondly, he had just arranged to have a landscaper clean up his yard and cancelled the work to deny the letter-writer a phony victory.

So, I wasn't *not* going to ask Alice to marry me this weekend just because Abby could crow.

Then, I opened up the right-hand drawer in my desk and took out my holster and gun and clipped them to my belt. The gun was a revolver, a .38 Special. I liked it because it only had five chambers, which made it a tad lighter to carry. I have other guns, including 9mm automatics with clips that hold up to 15 rounds, but I wasn't working a case and if I needed more than five shots to solve an unexpected problem, I don't deserve my Annie Oakley shooter's badge.

Of course, I always have six extra bullets in the holster slots, but that's just sensible, even if reloading during a surprise gunfight would be comical, and usually fatal.

My headstone would probably read: *He Died With His Boots On and One Bullet Left in His Holster*.

I had given some thought to how I would propose to Alice. I certainly didn't want to overdo it. We weren't going to a ball game so that thousands of people watching the Jumbotron would cheer and clap while I got down on my knees. For that matter, the knee thing was a non-starter no matter where we were.

I'd already made a reservation at Bin 5, a hot new restaurant that replaced the quirky but great Aesop's Tables in Rosebank. Not that I planned a proposal in a restaurant, either. With my luck, halfway through my declaration the waiter would wheel up a dessert cart.

Alice always liked to go to my house right from the ferry, to drop her stuff off and perhaps freshen up. So, when she walked into the house and saw the flowers on the table in my front parlor and the nice cold bottle of champagne, she'd turn to me and I'd be standing behind her with my little blue box.

The champagne! The flowers had been in a vase since the morning, but the bubbly was still in the refrigerator! Certainly cold, but hardly romantic. (*Hold that thought, honey. I've got to get something out of the fridge.*)

I looked at my watch again. I still had enough time to run home and put the champagne in an ice bucket.

***

I was halfway home when it occurred to me that I

didn't have an ice bucket. I used to have one, a nice red one, but I'd lent it to someone on my block. I didn't remember when, or to whom. I'd be damned if I would go around to all my neighbors and ask who had it. Probably the same person who had my rake, the one with all its tongs intact. The rake I had left has so many tongs missing it looks like the smile of the guitar kid in *Deliverance*.

I didn't want to borrow an ice bucket, either. Never a lender or borrower be, that's my motto now. I had a big aluminum tub that I filled with beer and soda for parties, but that wouldn't do. The sink was also out. I looked at my watch. Again. Good Lord, was I nervous?

The big box stores like Walmart or Target were on the other side of Staten Island, so I stopped in the Quaker Gift Shop on Castleton Avenue just around the corner from my house on St. Austin's Place in West Brighton. I knew the manager, Rita, well, since I made it a point to shop locally for gifts, although I guiltily also used my Amazon Prime account.

"What can I do for you, Alton," Rita said.

She seemed glad to see me, probably because, thanks to Amazon's predations, I was the only customer in her store.

"I was hoping you had an ice bucket."

"Is it a gift, or just for personal use?"

"Is there a difference?"

"Of course. If you want a metal ice bucket for use around the house, we have a few of them."

She turned her mouth down. Apparently, she didn't think much of metal ice buckets.

"But if it's for a gift, say for a wedding or housewarming, you'd obviously have to go crystal or sterling silver."

She smiled.

"But they are not inexpensive."

Rita had me. I'd be damned if I'd put Alice's champagne in a cheap tin ice bucket.

"It's a gift," I said.

We settled on a sterling silver ice bucket that looked like the Stanley Cup. Rita gave me a break, and it only cost a car payment. I'd shoot anyone who asked to borrow it.

Rita was full of questions about what kind of gift it was, who it was for, where it was going and the like. She offered to wrap it for me, and even ship it for a small fee. I told her it was part of a larger package and would take care of it myself. I finally extricated myself, feeling less guilty about Amazon.

When I got home, I endured Gunner's enthusiasm. He's a big dog, and no longer leaps to put his front paws on my shoulders. I had to break him of that habit after he decked a Jehovah's Witness.

But he can still lap up a storm when you bend down to his level. I opened the back door and he headed to his favorite tree. The house, a side-hall colonial I inherited from my parents, was spotless and smelled of Pine-Sol, or whatever Elie, the cleaning lady, used. I had her in a week earlier than usual, just for the occasion.

Take that, Abby.

I loved the place. It had memories and charm. And the neighborhood was both quirky and solid, not a bad combination.

But the plumbing and wiring were old. I'd replaced the original octopus furnace, which looked like one of the boilers on the Titanic, and put in central air. And new windows. And a roof. And new shingles. But something was always going wrong. Things broke that I didn't know the house even had.

Alice and I liked to work around the place, and did a lot of the repairs ourselves but it was getting too big for just a couple. It needed a complete makeover, and a family. Now, that was something that I didn't spend a lot of time thinking about. I wondered what Alice thought about that. Would she even want to live on Staten Island? She had an apartment and a life in Manhattan.

Maybe it was my imagination, but the blue box in my pocket suddenly felt heavier.

I shook my head. I was getting ahead of myself. I washed out the ice bucket and filled it with ice. It was a damn big bucket. I almost cleaned out the ice tray of my ice maker. I put the bottle of Veuve Cliquot Brut in the bucket.

My cell phone buzzed. I smiled. It was Alice. I suspected that she had missed the 4:20 ferry. All my rushing around and watch watching for naught. Well, it would give the ice maker some time to catch up.

It wouldn't be the first time Alice missed the ferry. She lives in Greenwich Village and packs minimally when coming to stay with me for a weekend, because we both leave casual clothes at each other's place. She'd have packed in the morning but would have taken a cab to Christopher Street to change and pick up the bag.

I told her once that it would save time and hassle if she went straight to the Staten Island Ferry from Barnard, which is uptown in Morningside Heights. She said she liked to do it her way, and I sensibly never brought it up again.

I think Alice likes to take the subway from the Village to South Ferry or the nearby Bowling Green station when she can, like a true New Yorker. Except, of course, that the New York Subway system is going through one of its periodic crises. Political finger pointing over who pays for what improvements is a lot more regular than train timetables.

One media wag suggested that the Governor and Mayor sit down and hash out their mass-transit differences on the subway tracks at Times Square, where they will be undisturbed by oncoming trains.

Of course, Alice missed ferries when she had plenty of time and when the subways were reliable. Anyway, I'd soon know why. One of the things I loved about her was that she would fess up.

"Hi," I said.

"Alton, it's Alice."

Alice knows that I have caller I.D. on my cell and would recognize her voice anywhere. I was surprised she identified herself. Then again, her voice did sound different.

Not enough to confuse me even if there was no caller I.D. … but with a different timber.

"What's wrong?"

"Kevin is dead," she said. "I can't believe it. He was so young."

CHAPTER 7 - NOEL

Kevin? My brain did a racing change as I went through a foggy mental list. It wasn't a parent, grandparent or uncle. People don't normally use first names when identifying such older family members. She didn't have a brother named Kevin.

Brother-in-law? Alice had a married sister, living in Boston. I met the sister once, briefly, when she came alone to New York for a girlie weekend with Alice.

I'd picked Maureen up at the airport in Newark and met Alice for a quick drink at the White Oak Tavern on Waverly Place before the sisters politely but firmly sent me on my merry way. Was Maureen's husband named Kevin? I couldn't remember.

God, I hoped it was just a friend, sad as that would be, and not one of Alice's two nephews. They were just kids and she doted on them.

"How young?" I said, inanely.

"Same age as I am," Alice said. "We both had birthdays the same month we were married, so we celebrated them together with our anniversary, although we only had a couple of anniversaries, of course."

Bingo! Her ex-husband. Kevin Allender. I almost blurted *Thank God!* Alice had once been Alice Allender. She went back to her maiden name after they split up.

I realized I had been holding my breath. I let it out slowly, and hopefully, inaudibly. Given the alternatives, a dead ex-husband wasn't the end of the world. Except for him, of course,

I probably would have forgotten Alice's married name but for the fact she had only recently let me read her unpublished book manuscript. *Opportunity*, by Alice Allender.

When we first met, Alice told me she wouldn't let me read it until she knew me better. Then, we both kind of forgot about it until a few months ago, when she found the manuscript at the bottom of a drawer she was cleaning out to donate some clothes to Goodwill. I was helping her and keeping my mouth shut about some of the clothes, which still had sale tags on them, when she gave me *Opportunity* to read.

Kevin had written a very encouraging comment on the manuscript cover. I thought the book was pretty good myself and said so. But my critique, while heartfelt and supportive, was not as effusive as his. They hadn't been married long, and he was no doubt still very much in love with Alice. Much as it galled me, I assumed he was a nice guy. And I thought "Alice Allender" was a great name for an author, although I didn't tell her that. Sleeping dogs and all that.

"How did you find out he died?"

"A San Francisco police detective called me."

I knew that they were called Inspectors in Frisco but didn't correct her. Not the time.

"What happened?"

"The detective said it was probably a suicide, but they were covering all the bases. My name was among some of Kevin's papers. And there was a picture of us, when we were married."

Probably?

"So, it might have been an accident?"

"No. The police said that while it's possible people could slip over the rail on their decks, they are pretty high. Besides, Kevin's body was too far from the building for him to have just fallen straight down."

There was a pause, and I heard an intake of breath.

"He landed in the pool."

That made the "probably" more interesting.

"How did the cops know where to find you?"

"From a Christmas card list. You knew we still exchanged cards."

I did know that. I thought it was a little weird, but Alice had told me their divorce was amicable, probably because there were no kids involved. She had even kept in touch with some of Allender's family, who apparently were still fond of her. Alice was the kind of person that people liked and would find hard to think ill of.

While she told me that neither she nor Kevin really were to blame for the marriage falling apart, I'd bet some of his relatives and friends thought he was nuts to lose her. I certainly thought so, even if I was grateful he did.

"Kevin was very organized," Alice said. "He liked his lists."

"What was the inspector's name?"

"Inspector?"

"I mean, detective."

"Hold on. I wrote it down."

There was a short pause, and then she said, "Charles Lin".

"Did he say how Kevin took his life."

There was another pause. I knew Alice was collecting herself. I waited.

"He said Kevin apparently jumped from the terrace of his apartment."

Although she is a good mimic and not above spearing the pretentious verbally, Alice never dramatizes what she says when being serious. So, I caught the slight inflection in her voice when she said 'apparently'.

"Apparently?"

"Actually, he used the term 'allegedly' once. When I asked him about it, he said it just slipped out."

I wondered about that. *Probably* and *apparently* might be innocuous, but cops are usually very careful with *allegedly*. Unless Lin was intentionally planting a seed of doubt. My spider sense kicked in. I wanted to ask Alice how he sounded when he said it. I had other questions as well, but now wasn't the time to ask them.

"How do you feel, honey?"

"Sad. Ambivalent. Confused. Angry. Hell, Alton, I don't know how I feel right now. Shocked, of course. I just can't see Kevin taking his own life. We had our differences, obviously, but he was never depressed."

I stated the obvious.

"People change," I said.

"I know. I know. And I haven't seen him in years."

"But you exchange Christmas cards."

For some reason, which probably said more about me than Alice, that bothered me a little. Of course, I didn't let Alice know that.

"I know that's always bothered you."

So much for hiding my feelings.

"Don't be silly."

What else could I say?

"It was just something I started, not Kevin. I mean, when we were married I sent cards to his sister and aunt. His parents are dead. And they sent them to me even after we divorced. We really got along. So, it just seemed natural to send him a card, too. And he responded. Our divorce was really amicable. I think the card thing was more rote on Kevin's part. I mean, the last couple had his name printed on them."

"Have you spoken to his family?"

"I called his sister, Rosemary. She lives in Tampa. She's very upset, of course. Kevin was her baby brother. She wants him buried in Tampa, since he has no relatives in San Francisco. No real ties, other than his job."

"He was in finance, if I recall."

"Still is. I mean was."

We were both silent for a moment, contemplating the eternal gulf between "is" and "was".

"He was a Wall Street guy, right? Merrill Lynch? When you were married."

"I'm surprised you remember that."

"I remember everything about you."

"That's sweet."

"I'm thinking of putting that word on my business card, to offset the skull and crossbones."

Alice laughed, which was good.

"Rosemary said Kevin left New York, and Merrill, a few years ago. Joined a boutique investment house in San Francisco that specializes in high-tech companies.

She said he was doing quite well."

I wanted to say that money wasn't everything. After all, I had Alice.

"Alton, I am going to the funeral."

"Did she ask you?"

"Not in so many words. But I can't imagine there will be many people there and I could tell it would make her happy."

"And you? Will it make you happy?"

"Yes. I really liked Kevin. He was a nice man. And part of my life."

"Then you should go."

There was a pause.

"I want you to go with me. Will you?"

I don't know where it came from, but I had the grace not to hesitate.

"Of course."

"Thank you."

"No need. Alice, you are part of my life. The most important part."

"I can't come for the weekend. I have to change my class schedule for next week, call colleagues to cover, and the like. And I was going to grade some papers on Monday. I feel I should go in and do them over the weekend. I'm sorry."

"I understand."

"I love you."

"I know. I love you, too."

"When I find out what the funeral arrangements are, I'll let you know."

"Sure."

We hung up. I hoped I had sounded both

supportive and not disappointed. I suspected I did better with the supportive part.

I took out the dark blue box. I opened the lid and looked at the ring for a long moment, and mouthed a phrase that I always thought trite, but knew to be true.

Life is what happens when you are making plans.

CHAPTER 8 - SLEEPING DOGS AND CATS

"Tampa? I thought you said he died in San Francisco."

Arman Rahm put a finger in his drink and put it in front of Gunner's snout. The dog sniffed it and then lapped the finger.

"That's where he worked. No family out West. His sister lives in Florida. She and Alice have always stayed in touch."

"How do you feel about it?"

"About what?"

"Going to the funeral of Alice's ex-husband."

"She asked me, so I'll go."

Gunner placed his head back in Arman's lap.

Gunner is a Byelorussian Ovcharka, or East European Shepherd, a mix of East Siberian Laika dogs and German Shepherds confiscated by the Russian Army from German territory at the end of World War II. As Arman once explained to me, the Red Army was by then short of war dogs, since earlier in the titanic battles of the Eastern Front desperate Russians had trained their existing animals to run under German tanks with explosives tied to their backs. The undercarriage of Nazi tanks was particularly vulnerable and the Germans lost a lot of tanks. And the Reds lost a lot of dogs.

The Ovcharka breed is noted for their loyalty, stamina, brute courage and superior intelligence. I'm pretty sure no Ovcharka would run under a tank.

The Russian Government gave two Ovcharka puppies to Marat Rahm, Arman's father, as a gift for something he did for the homeland. Since Marat was a former KGB bigwig who now was the patriarch of an American criminal organization, just what that was is shrouded in mystery. I never asked, and don't want to know.

The Rahms gave me one of the puppies. Actually, Arman offered Gunner to me in the presence of Alice, who immediately fell for the cute little fur ball. That sealed the deal, as I'm sure he knew it would. Gunner, named after a Medal of Honor winner whose murder I solved, is still cute according to Alice, but his fur ball days are long gone.

"But going to the funeral will make you feel uncomfortable."

Rahm recrossed his legs and absentmindedly scratched Gunner's ears. It was early Sunday evening. I'd called him to ask if I could drop off Gunner for a few days, to hang around with his litter mate. When the two big dogs got together, they ran around the Rahm property in tandem and looked like they should be chasing a sled through the snow on the Russian steppe.

Arman had said he was in his car and it would be easier if he just stopped by my house.

"It will be awkward. I'd rather let sleeping dogs lie. But I am curious to see what his family thinks about his alleged suicide."

"Alleged? You suspect foul play?"

"No real reason to. But Alice got a vibe from talking to the San Francisco cops. And I've learned not to ignore her vibes."

We were on the back deck of my house. Arman

and I were sitting at a small table drinking Jameson's. Maks Kalugin sat in a chair nearby drinking coffee. I'd offered him vodka, but he said he wanted coffee.

"Doctor's orders," Arman explained. "He has to cut back on the vodka."

I looked at the old killer.

"Problems?"

"Annual checkup," Maks snorted.

"All my people have a medical plan," Arman explained. "Annual checkups are included."

The Rahm's legitimate business empire had expanded into medical clinics and nursing homes. But I knew that even his less-than-savory employees got medical coverage. My friends in the District Attorney's office often complained to me that their insurance plan was inferior to that of thugs they prosecuted.

"Stupid policy," Kalugin said. "I felt fine."

I laughed.

"Did they make you go at gunpoint?"

"I take Marat for his checkup, and he makes me do it," Kalugin said, morosely.

The image of Maks Kalugin getting an annual physical, which undoubtedly included a prostate exam, filled me with joy.

"Next time, tell the doctor you want him to use two fingers, for a second opinion."

Kalugin looked confused, but Arman roared. Then, Kalugin got it. And gave me one finger.

"How is your father, Arman?"

Marat Rahm had been battling prostate cancer.

"Much better, thank you. He is in Italy, visiting

Eleni. And playing grandpa. She has a little boy now. Stephan."

"After your brother."

"Yes."

Stephan was Arman's older brother, assassinated years earlier. Eleni was Arman's actress sister, who soon after the murder had literally played a role that almost got me killed. But she also helped save my life and, in her way, was responsible for my relationship with the Rahm family.

"I didn't know she was married."

"She isn't."

"How old is the child?"

Rahm looked at me and then laughed.

"Oh, no. Don't worry. He's not yours. Too young. Father is some French actor she knew. He's out of the picture now. Eleni was always a free spirit. The boy is a delight."

The Rahms never held it against me that I slept with Eleni, who was pre-Alice. Probably because it furthered their scheme at the time, a scheme in which they betrayed me.

I couldn't hold the betrayal against them. They chose family over me. Blood is thicker than water. At least they stopped my bleeding when it came right down to it. It was only one of several times that Maks Kalugin saved my skin, something probably made more palatable for him because of his fondness for Alice. If I cheated on her now, with anyone, Kalugin would probably shoot me. Many times.

"What?" Rahm said.

"Huh?"

"You are shaking your head."

"Nothing."

Arman dipped his finger in his whiskey again and offered it to Gunner. This time there was no sniffing. Gunner went straight to lapping.

"Are you trying to get my dog drunk?"

"He's Russian. He can hold his liquor."

In the distance we could hear a siren. It seemed that was a more common occurrence recently. As if reading my thoughts, Rahm said, "Probably another drug overdose."

The opioid scourge was devastating rich and poor on Staten Island. Even before they legitimized most of their operations, the Rahms avoided the drug trade

"Staten Island is changing. A lot more crime than when we were growing up, Alton."

That comment, coming from a member of a family that controlled an empire that still depended on select criminality, begged for a sarcastic retort.

But I knew what he meant. In our youth, both the cops and mobsters frowned on what is now known as "street crime". The mob dumped plenty of bodies in the now-closed Fresh Kills landfill, but most of the corpses were imports. With a few exceptions, mobsters still only committed violence on each other. But there had been a few high-profile non-mob killings in recent years, some of which I was involved in. So, while Staten Island still had the lowest per-capita rates of violent crimes and burglaries in the city, the word "negligible" no longer applied.

"There's 300,000 more people living here than when we were kids, Arman."

"Many of whom came here to escape crime in other boroughs," he said. "Ironic, isn't it?"

We were suddenly joined on the deck by Scar, the huge and almost-feral tomcat that adopted me and maintained a wary truce with Gunner.

"A pity this suicide thing came up," Rahm said. "Just when you were going to ask Alice to marry you."

"What the hell! Is my love life on the damn internet?"

"No mystery, Alton. I own a piece of the jewelry store where you had the ring crafted. I understand it is quite beautiful."

Scar, whose affection for me was limited to the occasional small dead mammal he dropped at my feet, padded over to Kalugin and jumped in his lap. I was momentarily speechless as the cat curled up and started purring as Kalugin gently petted him.

"Kindred spirits," Arman said.

I poured us both a couple of more fingers of whiskey.

"You know, Maks," Aman said, "this Irish whiskey is not bad. You should try some, for medicinal purposes only, of course."

Kalugin nodded and held out his coffee mug. I walked over and poured some Jameson's into it. Annoyed at the interruption, Scar momentarily stopped purring, but resumed as I sat back in my chair.

"Want some whipped cream? A little nutmeg? I make a hell of an Irish coffee."

Kalugin grunted, then sipped his coffee.

"Who will watch the cat in your absence?" he asked.

"Scar is a free spirit," I said. "Neighborhood kid stops by to check on him."

"I presume the engagement is on hold," Arman said.

"Yes. It's not a good time for her."

"That will suit Maks. He does not believe you would make a suitable husband. He is very fond of Alice, as I am."

I looked at Kalugin. His broad, craggy face, the last thing many Rahm enemies saw, was impassive.

"So, what's your problem Maks?" I said with some annoyance.

Having my love life apparently discussed by everyone in town was bad enough, but having it generate the disapproval of someone who probably grew up with people who dated yaks was a bit much. Rahm was smiling. I wasn't.

"You are in a dangerous profession," Maks said. "People often try to kill you."

"You should know," I said. "You were once one of them."

Kalugin shrugged.

"Was that a 'sorry' shrug," I said, "or a 'should have' shrug?"

Maks gave me a rare smile and shrugged again.

"Don't pay any attention to Maks," Arman said. "If you are married and get yourself killed, Alice will benefit legally and financially."

"Thanks a lot."

"I hadn't thought about that," Kalugin said. "By all means, marry her."

"Are you guys having fun?"

Arman laughed.

"I like San Francisco," Rahm said. "Do you think you will have to go there?"

"I don't know. It will probably depend on what I learn at the funeral."

"If Alice wants you to go, you go," Kalugin said.

"I know people out there," Arman said. "Call me if you need help."

"Thanks, but I'm hoping I can wrap it up quickly."

"You are dreaming, my friend."

"What do you mean?"

"Will proving that her former husband killed himself make Alice happy?"

"No."

"Will proving that he was murdered make her happy?"

I could see where he was going.

"Either way would provide some sort of...", I couldn't think of a better word, so I used one I hated, "closure".

"I hate that word," Kalugin rumbled.

"I don't know why, Maks," I said. "It perfectly explains your life's work."

"Suicide or murder, you, being you, Alton, will want to find out the 'why'," Arman continued, "because Alice will want to know."

"You are fucked," Kalugin said.

My thoughts exactly.

CHAPTER 9 - TAMPA

The Airbus 320 bucked in the slight turbulence of a rain shower as we banked into Tampa International Airport. Alice tightened her hand on my arm. She was a good flier, but the jolt had surprised her.

"Sorry," she said.

I smiled and hoped she hadn't noticed the white knuckles on my hands. I know the science behind manned flight. Air flow over the wing, pressure variances, thrust, and the like. I'm even willing to trust the aerodynamic eggheads when a 75-ton jetliner leaves the ground.

But that doesn't mean I have to like it. After all, scientists argue that a bumblebee shouldn't fly, but it does. It didn't help that the previous night, while channel surfing, I watched a cable show entitled *Why Airplanes Crash*. It featured a jetliner that plowed into the ground short of a runway because its autopilot was receiving faulty data from a computer. I made a conscious effort to relax my grips on the armrests.

A moment later the pilot, or maybe the computer (!) that was doing the actual flying, adjusted the wing slats and lowered the wheels. An Airbus has less sound-proofing than a Boeing, so Alice and I both expected the thumps and whines that accompanied those activities, so we weren't startled. In any event, they were preferable to the normal landing noises made by some military aircraft I'd flown. On my first flight on a C-130 during basic training I assumed we were crashing. And from the looks on most of the other recruits who were web-strapped to the sides of the plane, I was not alone in that assumption.

Now, with nary a bump, we landed in sunshine on what appeared to be a dry runway. Florida weather is not only unpredictable, but seemingly changes from one zip code to the next.

With only carry-on luggage and a garment bag that the flight attendant stored for us on a hanger in the front of the plane, we got to the Avis counter quickly, where an agent apologized for his lack of sedans.

"Everyone wants an SUV nowadays," he said.

So, we drove into Tampa proper in a new Jeep Cherokee. The highway was indeed full of SUVs. I wasn't crazy about the new trend. I like to see what's ahead of the vehicle in front of me, and that was a lot easier to do when sedans ruled the road. Somehow, I suspected that so-called "driver-less" vehicles wouldn't help matters. Driver-less cars? Computer-controlled planes? I love technology as much as the next guy, but sometimes it gave me pause.

"What?"

It was Alice.

"Huh?"

"You said, 'Good Lord'."

"I did?"

"You did."

"I must have been talking in my sleep."

"While driving?"

"These new cars are amazing, aren't they?"

"It's an SUV."

"I rest my case."

She shook her head and went back to reading the tourist brochure she'd picked up at the airport.

I had to admit that the Cherokee drove like a dream. It was unlike the jeeps I recalled from my military days. This one had leather motorized seats, an entertainment console that looked like it belonged on the Space Shuttle and so many bells and whistles that I had immediately opened the glove box to read the owner's manual.

The glove box was empty. The manual was probably too big to fit in it, and I was left on my own. I suspected that the Cherokee had a built-in GPS system but rather than pushing the wrong button and ejecting Alice or launching cruise missile at Moscow, I used the GPS on my smart phone. A half hour later, after a smooth, silent ride that would have humiliated a military jeep, we pulled into the parking lot of the Versailles Palace, one of Tampa's oldest hotels.

I had stayed at the Versailles Palace many years before, and it had not aged well. It was getting so that you couldn't even trust website photos.

We both dodged some workmen who were painting the lobby. The website had not mentioned anything about renovations.

"I think the Palace has seen better days," I said.

"From the look of the carpet," Alice added, "better centuries would have been more appropriate."

But the young receptionist, a perky blond, was friendly. After explaining that the venerable hotel would soon be restored to its former glory, she happily upgraded my reservation to a junior suite at no extra charge.

"The restaurant is closed for renovations," she said, adding chirpily, "but the bar is open!"

I resisted a "thank God". None of it was the kid's fault.

"If you leave your bags, I'll have someone bring them to your room. One of our elevators is out, but Mario should be back at any moment."

"Not necessary," I said. "We can manage on our own. But thank you, Wendy."

That was the name on the name tag perched precariously over her ample right breast.

One of the elevators was being worked on. A technician had just removed the panel outside the elevator and said, "Oh, boy." I saw a tangle of wires, some of which looked like they had been installed by Thomas Edison.

"Must have been tough redoing all the wiring on this one," I said, pointing to the elevator that we were going to use.

"Haven't gotten to that one yet," he said.

Wonderful. If my upgrade hadn't put us on the 14th floor, I would have headed for the stairs. I punched the button for our floor and the doors closed.

"There is no 13th floor," Alice noted, pointing to the inside panel.

"An old superstition," I said.

"Of course, we are on what is actually the 13th floor."

I wished she hadn't mentioned that.

"You couldn't take your eyes off that girl's chest," Alice said.

"I wanted to make sure I got her name right."

"Of course. 'Wendy' is hard to remember."

"It wasn't that. The name tag was so close to my

face that some of the letters were outside my vision."

It was good to hear Alice laugh.

The room, or rather, the "Junior Suite", turned out a lot better than I'd expected. It was old, as were its furnishings, but it was clean and roomy. The bathroom was spotless.

"Charming," Alice said, without a trace of sarcasm.

It is the rare hotel room I'm in with a beautiful woman and an inviting king bed that my actions don't immediately turn carnal.

"We have just enough time to shower, dress and grab a quick bite before we have to be at the funeral home," Alice said.

This was, obviously, one of those rare hotel rooms.

"You should take the first shower," Alice said. "That way, I can dawdle."

It was hard to argue with someone who would come out looking so beautiful post-dawdle.

"Sure," I said.

I wondered if a cold shower really worked.

Afterward, I got dressed while Alice disappeared into the bathroom. I knocked on the door. She opened it wearing only a towel.

"I'm going downstairs to rustle up some chow," I said.

My voice was a little hoarse.

"See if you can rustle up a couple of beers, cowboy."

I took a chance on the elevator. The cable held. When I got out of the car, the same technician was still working on the same panel, which now looked like a mare's nest.

"Whatever you do," I said, "don't cut the red wire!"

"Huh?"

"Nothing, just a little N.C.I.S. humor."

I went to the reception desk. Wendy beamed. I tried not to stare. I asked her where I could get a couple of sandwiches nearby.

"There a nice little place around the corner on Cass Street. If you like Cuban food."

"I could eat Raul Castro right now."

Wendy giggled, and gave me directions.

"Go out the door you came in, make a left and then another left at the light. The cafe is halfway up that block on your side. You can't miss it. Will you need directions coming back?"

"If I make a right, and a right, will I be safe?"

"Oh yes, what was I thinking."

She giggled again.

Wendy might not have been the brightest bulb in the chandelier, but she knew her Cuban cafes. I bought two Cuban sandwiches and four bottles of ice-cold La Tropical, which the guy behind the register said came from a brewery in Miami but was an exact match of the real stuff from Cuba.

"Just got back from Havana myself," he said. "I can't tell the difference."

Alice was in a hotel robe putting on her makeup when I got back to the room.

"I didn't want to get dressed before we ate," she explained.

I was pretty sure there was nothing under the robe,

except Alice, of course. I tried to think about the Knicks.

The sandwiches were good, and the beer even better. Alice only wanted half a sandwich, and one beer. I wish I could say there were leftovers, but there weren't. I really could have eaten Raul Castro.

CHAPTER 10 - REPAST

The Braxton & Braxton Home for Funerals was handling Kevin Allender's final passage. Close family and friends gathered at 9 AM. Allender's sister, Rosemary, had asked Alice to be there. She was greeted warmly. Alice introduced me to Rosemary, her husband and their children, as well as a few other people I quickly forgot, but after that no one paid me much attention, which was fine with me.

I don't like funeral homes. I don't like the way they smell or look, or what they stand for. I ambled out to an adjacent waiting room, where a montage of pictures of the deceased were on an easel. A tabletop video projection of photos, many of which seemed to be copies of those on the easel, looped continuously. It had a soothing soundtrack, which I knew but couldn't identify. I hate when that happens and I thought about asking someone what it was, but it seemed borderline inappropriate, so I refrained.

From the photos, a few of which contained Alice, I noted that Allender wasn't a bad-looking fellow. I wouldn't have expected any less of a man Alice was involved with. Ahem.

I wondered what Allender looked like now. Probably not too spiffy, considering how he died, not to mention the transportation involved in getting him cross-country. The casket was closed.

The funeral director, who looked like a funeral director from central casting, led everyone in a small prayer recitation and then asked us to get in our cars.

There was a big red card under my wiper that said,

"FUNERAL". I put it on the dash and, herded by the funeral home staff, followed the line of cars to St. John the Evangelist, a Catholic church about a mile away on the same street. The church itself was all angles, glass and spires, and looked new. As always when entering a tax-break property, I wondered how much it cost.

We were all seated when the casket and pallbearers came down the aisle about 15 minutes later, to be greeted by a young and handsome Hispanic priest, flanked by two bored-looking altar boys.

I turned to Alice.

"A mass?"

She nodded.

"Was Kevin very religious?"

"I know he went to parochial school through high school, but when I knew him he wasn't religious at all. I guess he could best be described as agnostic. I remember that bothered his sister, who was very religious."

Kevin's agnosticism didn't mean much. The tugs of morality ingrained in childhood are strong, even among the lapsed.

When everyone was seated, the priest introduced himself and addressed the crowd.

"It's not often we have a service where the non-Catholics outnumber the Catholics," he said, to polite laughter. I wondered what he meant. "But all God's children are very welcome and appreciated. We are going to be offering Holy Communion and if you want to participate but don't want to take the host or wine, I would ask you to come forward and cross your hands over your chest and say a small prayer instead."

With that he began the service. His homily was generic, which was to be expected since Kevin Allender was basically a stranger to the parish. After Communion and some other prayers, the priest asked if anyone would like to say a few words. Allender's sister went to the pulpit and spoke briefly and eloquently about her brother, offering a few humorous sibling anecdotes about their teen years. She ended by reading a poem by Yeats and sat down. Alice wiped a tear from her eye. I gave her a handkerchief and patted her hand.

The service ended quickly after that and we headed to the cemetery. I hadn't thought to enter the name of the cemetery into my rental car's GPS system. I dislike funeral processions, especially when there are traffic circles involved. And we hit perhaps 10 of them on the way to Kevin Allender's final resting place, 20 minutes away. I came close to needing my own plot after being cut off by distracted drivers in a couple of circles, which locals called "roundabouts". I called them something else, until Alice punched me in the arm. So much for "FUNERAL" placards.

The service at the grave site was brief. A few more prayers and the priest sprinkled some holy water on the casket. Mourners placed roses on it. Two workers, trying but failing to look properly respectful, stood next to a backhoe. It was pleasantly warm, and breezy.

Then the funeral director asked if anyone needed directions back to Grace Episcopal, where there would be a small repast. Alice saw my confusion.

"Rosemary also fell away from the Catholic Church," she explained. "But she converted and is very devout. Grace Episcopal is her church. I thought it very nice that she would have Kevin's service in the religion in which he grew up."

This time I plugged the name into the GPS app. As we exited the cemetery, one of the Braxton & Braxton staffers politely asked for our "FUNERAL" signs. We were on our own, which suited me fine. As far as I could tell, the signs only served to alert other drivers so they could cut me off in a roundabout.

***

Grace Episcopal was an older church, but it and other parish buildings sat on what appeared to be several acres of land. Religion is big business in the South.

The repast was in a large facility that housed both a school and a cafeteria. The hallway walls leading to the cafeteria were lined with drawings and posters made by schoolchildren. Trays of Sterno-warmed food were set out on a long table in the back of the cafeteria, tended by smiling women. There were also cold cuts and various salads, and trays of cookies and cakes, which looked home-made.

Round tables of 10 began to fill up, and there was chatter and laughter, subdued at first, and then louder, as people greeted one another and began reminiscing. I looked around in vain for a station with wine or beer, and only found a small table with coffee, lemonade, soft drinks, water and iced tea.

Neither Alice or I was hungry, but I got us coffee, and we sat at a table with Rosemary. Next to her was an elderly woman who looked like Angela Lansbury. I'd spotted her in church. Alice had identified her as

"Aunt Maggie". I didn't know which side of Allender's family she came from, but from the way everyone deferred to her, I gathered she was an institution. There was a walker, folded up, leaning against her chair. She was direct, acerbic, irreverent and feisty. We hit it off immediately.

"I heard about you, young man. Alice's fella. A detective. You here to detect something?"

"I'm just supporting Alice. She was very fond of Kevin, and his family."

Aunt Maggie was sipping coffee. She looked at her plate, which had an assortment of salad, Swedish meatballs, chicken something and mashed potatoes.

"This crap isn't much better than what I get at the nursing home," she said. "They don't know how to serve it hot, either. And Rosemary always forgets to get me a dessert. How about getting me some cookies and one of those lemon squares they always have at these things?"

"Be my pleasure."

I left her talking to Alice and Rosemary. I piled a plate full of dessert.

"They're for someone else," I explained to the ladies at the dessert stand.

"Of course, they are," one of them said.

Back at the table, Aunt Maggie forced me to eat a chocolate chip cookie. Well, perhaps forced isn't the word. Anyway it, and my second one, were delicious.

Aunt Maggie only picked at her food, although she made a good dent on the desserts.

"At least the dessert isn't a damn sheet cake. I think all they do is change the icing."

We were interrupted by several people who stopped to talk to Rosemary and Aunt Maggie. Alice was introduced as Kevin's ex-wife, and I was her "friend". Everyone was very nice, their sincerity obvious.

My earlier cynical ruminations about tax exemptions and big church buildings, which had weakened amid the kids' posters in the hallways, felt even more churlish. These were nice, moral people, brought together by a common need to support bereaved friends.

Alice asked me if I'd get more coffee for her and Maggie. When I returned to the table, they were deep in conversation, both hands in each other's.

Aunt Maggie looked at me and smiled.

"Alice has been kind enough to offer to take me to dinner."

"That's nice," I said, wondering what was up.

"Kevin didn't kill himself, you know."

CHAPTER 11 — BERN'S

We drove Aunt Maggie to her nursing home. I parked in a small lot and snapped her walker together, which was a lot harder than it looked at first glance. I have the same trouble with beach chairs. I've been told that I often look as if I'm having a seizure when I try to open one of them.

After we helped Maggie out of the car, Alice and I both accompanied her to the front entrance of the two-story brick building, where a smiling Hispanic attendant held the door for her.

"I can make it from here. Manny will help me. He's legal, by the way."

"My pleasure Miss Maggie," the man said, winking at me.

"You can have my dinner Jell-O, Manny. I've got a date."

She turned to us.

"Now listen you two, there's no reason to spend a lot of money tonight. A Bob Evans just down the street that will do me fine."

The nursing home food must be really dreary.

"I was hoping we could take you to Bern's," I said. "It's supposed to be one of the best steakhouses in the country."

"Bern's," Aunt Maggie said. "I'd love to go there. Haven't been in years. But it would be wasted on me. Like I said, I eat like a bird."

"What we don't eat I'm sure we can bring back here," I said. "Place must have a refrigerator. The food won't go to waste, right Manny?"

"You bet," he said.

You just can't walk into Bern's," the old lady said. "They are booked weeks in advance."

"Just let me worry about that," I said.

Alice looked at me, with an expression that said, "don't promise what you can't deliver."

I soldiered on.

"What time would be good for you, Aunt Maggie?"

"Well, we eat early here. They start serving at 5 o'clock sharp. Some of the really old folks are barely waking up from their lunch naps. But I don't care what time I eat at Bern's. I haven't had a good steak in years. Be a chance to try out my new teeth. Jell-O is not much of a challenge."

***

Alice and I headed back to the hotel. Breakfast had been coffee in our room, and, other than more coffee and some cookies at the repast, neither of us had eaten. We stopped along the waterfront at Four Green Fields, which advertised itself as "America's Only Authentic Thatched-Roof Irish Pub".

I was ready to eat the thatch, but with Bern's hopefully in our future, we settled for soda bread and Irish Potato Leak soup. Alice had an iced tea, and I downed a pint of Guinness. I don't know about the thatch, but the pint was the real deal.

Later, back in our room, I called Bern's and asked for a table for three people at 7 P.M., which I knew would be an impossibility. I was put on hold, as expected.

I was sitting up in bed. Alice was next to me and

scrunched up higher on her pillows. We were both naked, although she had modestly covered herself with a sheet, which now slipped just below her breasts, which were still flushed, with hard nipples. Our lovemaking had been intense, with Alice particularly energetic.

I ascribed her enthusiasm to her gratitude at my making the trip with her, combined with a perhaps subconscious effort on her part to reassure me that she had no lingering feelings for her ex-husband. Whatever the reasons, they worked for me.

A nice young woman at Bern's came on the phone and asked me if I had a reservation.

"Not a one," I said, staring at Alice's bosom.

"Pardon me?"

"I'm sorry. No, I don't."

I always wondered why they always asked if I had a reservation, when it was obvious from my initial request that I didn't.

"I know it's a long shot. But I'm only in town for a couple of days. In fact, I'm flying out tomorrow and I want to take my clients out someplace special, and everyone says that in Tampa that means Bern's. I'm hoping someone may have canceled."

"Good Lord," Alice said.

I shushed her. It was a strategy I'd used often at restaurants where people usually have to make reservations weeks in advance. There are always cancellations, particularly on weeknights. A kid gets sick. Couples have a spat. The babysitter forgot the night. And most people who revere a restaurant like Bern's will call to cancel, rather than just not show up.

They don't want to get on the bad side of management.

My ploy almost always worked, except at the smaller "in" city restaurants that catered to celebrities and had a regular clientele. Bern's was a great steakhouse, but it was in Tampa, after all. I didn't expect to run into any paparazzi. And there was no reason I wouldn't have a client in a walker.

"Three people, you said."

"Yes."

There was a pause, which when dealing with reservations is almost always a positive sign.

"I'm afraid I can't do 7." No surprise there. A pause. "But I have openings at 5:45 and 8:15."

I assumed Aunt Maggie would appreciate nursing-home time, meal wise, so I chose 5:45. I certainly didn't want her falling asleep in the middle of a Porterhouse.

I called her and said I'd pick her up at 5. She was thrilled, which made me feel very good.

"Nicely, done," Alice said. "Just the right blend of groveling and lies."

"Anything for a business client," I said.

She kissed me and her hand slid down my stomach.

"Then let's get down to business," she said huskily.

Her hand didn't stop at my stomach. Soon, I was feeling very, very good.

***

We were a little early for dinner but weren't shunted to the bar when the staff saw Aunt Maggie's walker. We were quickly, and pleasantly, shown to a quiet table in one of the smaller alcoves that Bern's is noted for. The lighting was subdued, highlighting the paintings on the wall depicting various hunt scenes with lots of dogs and red-capped men and women on horses.

"This reminds me of a grotto," Alice said.

I asked our waiter for a wine list.

"Could I have a drink first," Aunt Maggie said.

"Of course."

She turned to the waiter.

"Beefeater martini, straight up, with two olives, the ones with the cheese inside. I want it very cold, and very dry. Don't bruise the gin with more than a drop of vermouth."

"Yes, ma'am," he said, smiling and turned to me.

I suppressed a laugh and looked at Alice, who nodded in amusement.

"Make it three," I said.

"You probably thought I'd order a nice little dry sherry," Aunt Maggie said as the waiter walked away. "Or a Bailey's." She winked. "That's for after dinner." A pause. "And after the wine."

At Bern's, there is every cut of steak available, in every thickness, and cooked to any color. Alice and I were looking at the menus the waiter had dropped off. Aunt Maggie just sat there, sipping her martini.

"Do you need help with the menu, Aunt Maggie? Would you like me to order for you?"

"Not necessary, sonny. I'm in an assisted-living home. I haven't been lobotomized. I went on line this afternoon and checked it out. I know just what I want."

In the end, she ordered a Delmonico, rare, with

French onion soup, a small Caesar Salad and a baked potato. Alice and I split a large Porterhouse, with the same sides. The wine list looked like a phone book, with choices up to $4,000 a bottle. I ordered a modestly priced Clos Pegase Cabernet. The waiter suggested that we take a tour of the restaurant's "famous wine cellar" after dinner.

"That wine list is only a sampling. We have 490,000 bottles in the cellar."

The thought of Aunt Maggie and her walker amid millions of dollars of wine bottles was a frightening thought.

"We'll see," I said.

"No, we won't," Maggie interjected. "I'm more interested in the dessert room upstairs. They have an elevator."

CHAPTER 12 - SURPRISE

The room upstairs was divided into many smaller alcoves which reminded me of old-style phone booths, only much larger. The after-dinner menu would have done Louis the Fourteenth proud, and we ordered two desserts to share, the Bourbon Bread Pudding and an English Trifle. Alice and I ordered coffee and Courvoisier. I looked at Aunt Maggie.

"Sherry?"

"I think I'd like an Irish Coffee," she said, turning to the waitress. "With Jameson's. But make it decaf. My health, you know."

I needn't have worried about Aunt Maggie falling asleep at dinner. I was the one having trouble keeping my eyes open.

"Now Alton," Aunt Maggie said when she got her Irish Coffee, "I guess it's time I sing for my supper."

She patted the large "doggie bag" on the table. The nursing home residents and staff would be very happy.

"Alice tells me you need some convincing that our Kevin didn't kill himself."

"That's not quite what I said, Aunt Maggie," Alice interjected.

"I know, I know. But that's what you meant. You have your suspicions, as do I. But you don't want to send your detective fellow off on some wild goose chase. I get that."

The old lady looked at me.

"What's your gut say?"

I sipped my brandy.

"Well, from everything I heard at the service, and

from what Alice has told me, suicide seems out of character."

"But there is no proof, otherwise? Of foul play, as they say? And Alice told me they have ruled out an accident."

"That's correct," I said.

Something was on Aunt Maggie's mind. She took a spoonful of trifle, then some pudding. Then a sip of her Irish Coffee, which left a small line of whipped cream on her upper lip. I was about to say something about it when she licked it off.

I waited. With the elderly, it's often the only thing to do while they gathered their thoughts. Of course, you always ran the risk that those thoughts would disappear. I didn't think that would be the case with Maggie. She was sharp as a tack and was probably being both careful and dramatic. She had an audience that wasn't drooling into their oatmeal, and she wanted to make the most of it.

"I don't think Kevin would kill himself just before his sister's wedding anniversary."

"Wedding anniversary?"

"Yup. A big one. Her 25th. Silver, right?"

"You didn't tell me that, Alice," I said.

"I didn't know until Rosemary mentioned it this morning. Is it important?"

"Probably not. Except sometimes family occasions, especially big ones, affect people in strange ways. Maybe rekindles memories. Feelings of things not done. Isolation. That sort of thing. It's not unheard of that a depressed person might commit suicide at such a time."

"Aww, bullshit," Aunt Maggie said vehemently.

At that, our waitress, who was approaching our table, pirouetted and left the room.

"Why do you say that?" I asked mildly.

"Because me and Kevin were planning a surprise anniversary party for Rosemary!"

"Surprise party?" both Alice and I said in unison.

"Yup. Scheduled for next week. I guess we can still have it. Be a bit subdued now. But life goes on, right? Anyway, we had the perfect cover, I think you'd call it. I'm in a home but have all my marbles and plenty of time on my hands. I was calling all over town. Planning the food. Inviting people. A deejay. That kind of stuff. Kevin was going to surprise his sister by showing up with a video, like the one at his funeral, with photos of his sister before and after the marriage. I already arranged the video machine, or whatever they call it."

Aunt Maggie took another spoonful of bread pudding.

"Rosemary and Marty, that's her husband, take me out to dinner every Sunday, to Season's 52. Love that place. They have rooms for small parties. And you can get a drink. Not like that goody-two-shoes church where we were just at. It was all set up. I've been sending photos out to Kevin for a year. I've been around a while. I had lots. Last I spoke to him, maybe a week ago, he was all excited about how the video came out. He said it had a great soundtrack of all the songs Rosemary loved. That was his bag, you know, tech stuff."

Aunt Maggie took a triumphal swig of her coffee,

this time getting some cream on the tip of her nose.

"Now, Mr. Detective, does that sound like someone who was going to kill himself?"

***

"Don't be a stranger, missy," Aunt Maggie said as she hugged Alice at the front door of the nursing home.

"I won't. I promise."

Maggie gave me a hug, too, and whispered in my ear.

"He didn't kill himself."

Then with her food packages consigned to an attendant, and her walker clacking away, she went inside.

On the drive back to our hotel, Alice said, "What do you think?"

"That I should go to San Francisco."

"Are you sure?"

"A lot of suicide denial is wishful thinking, Alice. But between you and Aunt Maggie, my spider sense is tingling. I think I want to talk to that detective. He probably doesn't know about the surprise party. What's his name again?"

"Lin. Charles Lin. I'll give you his number. He asked me to call him if I thought of anything. I wish I had known about the party when I spoke to him."

"I think you should call him. Don't mention the surprise party but vouch for me. Tell him that he can check me out with the D.A.'s office in Staten Island if he wants."

"I remember when you were persona non grata with everyone there, except Cormac."

"Politics and coverups make strange bed fellows."

"Part of me hoped it would be a wild goose chase," Alice said. "Kevin killed himself. But another part of me now hopes he was murdered. God. Does that make me a terrible person?"

"Either way, honey, you are not a terrible person. You are a wonderful woman, and just conflicted. A murder can, in some cases, be more dignified."

Alice looked at me.

"Perhaps I could have phrased that better. What I mean…"

"I know exactly what you mean, and you are right." She sighed. "What a crappy world this is."

"It's the world we live in. Anyway, I'll grab a flight to the coast tomorrow."

"Right away? You hardly have any clothes."

"I'll probably only be there a day or two. Just long enough to light a fire under the local fuzz if I find something suspicious. And if I have to stay longer, I'll just buy stuff. Besides, all Jack Reacher needs is a toothbrush when he travels around the country solving crimes and killing bad guys. I don't even think he changes his underwear."

"That's fiction, Alton."

I thought about the results of my last two trips to California. No fiction writer could do them justice. It made me wonder about my reception at the San Francisco Police Department. Law enforcement agencies talk to each other all the time.

I decided to hedge my bets and also call Jackie Noyce in Sonoma.

CHAPTER 13 - 'INSPECTOR' LIN

"Did you have a nice flight?"

Inspector Charles Lin handed me back my I.D.

"Plane took off and landed," I said. "I always consider that a nice flight."

"I got a call about you, Rhode. A Captain Noyce in the Sonoma County Sheriff Office."

"Jackie has always been a big fan of mine," I said. "Sure."

"I figured you might be more amenable to talk with me if you knew I wasn't a total yahoo."

"She said you were in the yahoo hall of fame," Lin said. "But you were usually on the right side of things and I could trust you. Pretty impressive coming from a cop who watched you shoot one of her officers in the squad room." Lin paused. "During his fucking retirement party."

"She tell you about that?"

"Hell no. But every cop in California knows about it."

"Actually, it was in her office. And he was a serial killer and a maniac."

"Why do you think I'm talking to you? You carrying a piece now?"

"I had to check it downstairs. Even after I showed my carry permit."

Lin smiled.

"Like I said, every cop in California. Let me see the permit."

I showed it to him. It identified me as a working member of the District Attorney's squad on Staten

Island. Which I wasn't. But when you save the D.A.'s career and the memory of his dead wife, there are certain perks.

"Who did you blow to get this?"

Lin handed the permit back to me.

"I found it in a fortune cookie."

Lin scowled.

"You making fun of my heritage?"

"You're Chinese? Sorry. I thought you were Japanese. Maybe Vietnamese. Eskimo?"

A fat black cop at the next desk started laughing.

"Yeah, all the gooks look alike, right Charlie?"

"Shut up, dickhead."

"I think we found a chink in his armor," the fat cop said.

That was quick and we all laughed. Insults are usually the way to cops' hearts, not political correctness. Lin, still smiling, looked at me.

"You're not going to shoot me, too, are you?"

I held up the coffee he'd given me when I sat and nodded at his cup.

"Won't have to. This stuff will kill you."

We were sitting at Lin's desk in the third-floor squad room of one of the strangest-looking police precinct houses I'd ever seen. The five-story square building was set on Vallejo Street, a narrow commercial block, and was flanked by bodegas, Asian restaurants and other small businesses, most of which had apartments in the brownstone-like structures they occupied. The police station itself had a street-to-roof facade that looked like hundreds of dominoes stacked on top of each other.

The domino-look in a notorious earthquake zone made me nervous.

"I didn't think the coffee could be as bad as this building's architecture," I said. "I was wrong."

"No argument there. Guy who built this place must have been on drugs. But this is the best station in the city. I can walk three blocks in any direction and find great food."

"Amen to that," the cop at the next desk said.

Cops don't care what their precinct looks like, inside or out. As long as they can get a good meal somewhere.

"So, what's your interest in Allender?" Lin said.

I told him.

"That's tough. I spoke to your lady on the phone. She seemed like a nice woman. Why is she suspicious?"

"Nothing specific. She just doesn't think her ex-husband was the suicidal type."

Lin shook his head.

"People change."

"I know. But we spoke to some of Allender's kin at the funeral and they were stunned that he would take his own life."

I had decided to keep Aunt Maggie's revelation about the surprise party to myself until I found out more. I wanted to see what Lin thought before I sent him off on a tangent.

Lin shrugged.

"Same answer."

"Look. I don't like stepping on anyone's toes. But I also don't like going through the motions. I told

Alice I'd find out what happened. So, I have to ask you, is there anything about this case that bothers you?"

Lin looked at me. I could see what he was thinking. Did I just question his competency? After all, the death was ruled a suicide.

"We went through the guy's apartment. And through his computer."

"The alleged suicide note was on the screen?"

Lin let the "alleged" go.

"Yes. There were no signs of a struggle. Bruises on the body and head were consistent with the fall, even if he hadn't hit the diving board. A belly flop from 12 floors, the M.E. says, isn't a walk in the park. Lots of trauma. Face was mashed pretty good. The apartment was a little messy, but the guy lived alone. There was even a little dog shit on the carpet."

"What happened to his dog?"

"I didn't say he had a dog. He didn't. You can't walk anywhere in this city without stepping in dog shit. He probably tracked it in."

That didn't jibe with what Alice had told me about Allender. She said he was fastidious.

"Did you check his shoes?"

Lin saw where I was going.

"His shoes were spotless. But they were in the pool. The water probably cleaned whatever was on them. They had to drain the pool, and not only because of possible dog poop. There was blood and other bodily fluids. Dead men leak, you know."

"Yeah. How about security cameras?"

"Not installed yet. Building has a guard all night at

the front desk. Long-time employee. Said no one came into the building after about 1 A.M."

"He never left the desk? Even to take a leak?"

"Sure he did. And locked the front door when he went to the can. Put one of those 'Be Right Back' signs on the door when he did."

"You believe him?"

"No reason not to. Like I said. Long-time employee. No record."

"Any other way in?"

"Back door is locked at all times. You have to swipe a key to gain access. Door was secure. No sign of forced entry. Same with Allender's apartment door. That, you need a regular key for. But it was locked, too."

I had to admit, Lin had been thorough. He picked up a smart phone from his desk and continued as he scrolled through it.

"Allender worked in a high-tech, high-pressure industry." He started reading from his notes. "Small firm called Allender Financial Research. Specialized in block chains and cryptocurrency."

He looked up.

"Don't ask me about it. I'm not sure I'd know what I'm talking about. All mumbo-jumbo to me. Just another way to separate people from their money."

Lin looked at his notes again, and then put the phone down.

"He was a bit of a loner at work, but the people he employed said he was a nice guy. They all appeared stunned by the news. Said he was a bit withdrawn lately, and was a workaholic, but that's par for the course in their world. Might have drank too much on occasion. Did the occasional joint. I mean, this is San Francisco."

"Anything stronger?"

"If he did, it didn't pop up in the tox screen. He was pretty waterlogged, and that can screw up forensics a bit. And no booze in his system the night he did the Brodie."

I smiled.

"I haven't heard that term in a while. Brodie jumped off the Brooklyn Bridge."

"We get a lot of jumpers here, too, as you might have heard. Anyway, everything points to suicide. And it's like what they say about serial killers. Gee, he looked so normal."

"What was he wearing?"

"Why do you want to know?"

"I don't know. Just curious, I guess."

"He was fully clothed. Jacket and tie. The works. Brooks Brothers, if it matters."

"So, his work clothes. At that hour?"

Lin shrugged.

"A lot of suicides dress up before they off themselves. Make a statement. Also, many don't want to be found in their skivvies. And maybe he was so depressed he just sat around after work and never changed."

"So, nothing bothers you."

Lin paused.

"The scream. Maybe."

"Scream?"

"Guy in the building with a bad prostate was up

taking a leak. Heard a splash in the pool that was probably caused by the vic. Also thought he heard a scream, though he won't swear to it. Bothered me a bit. Most suicide jumpers don't scream."

"Maybe Allender changed his mind on the way down."

"Possible. But a 12-floor drop goes pretty quick. Not much time to change your mind."

"So, maybe the drop wasn't Allender's idea."

"And maybe the witness didn't hear a scream at all. Old guy. And his wife said it might have been someone screaming on the TV."

"Did you check if anyone else heard a scream?"

Lin stared at me. I could have kicked myself.

"Sorry. I know you checked. But did anyone else hear it?"

He let my bad manners slide.

"No. Most people in other apartments were asleep, and those that weren't had their sliders shut. It was a cool night, like most around here this time of year. The only reason my witness might have heard something is because he had his slider open. I asked around the neighborhood, same thing. Nobody heard nothin'."

Lin was a good cop. Thorough. Professional.

"Anything else, Inspector?"

He paused.

"The computer."

"The suicide note?"

"No. That was boilerplate. He said he was lonely. Overworked. Not getting anywhere in his business. A failure. Yada, yada, yada. I've seen a dozen notes like it. And a lot on computer screens. It's the modern thing for tech and financial guys. I doubt some of them can even write cursive."

"Then, what bothers you?"

"Well, it was a powerful laptop, only a few years old. And there wasn't all that much on it, file and doc wise. Lots of family photos, including a video presentation. I would have expected more stuff, especially from a Wall Street guy."

"Was it wiped?"

Lin shrugged.

"Who knows? And who's to say he didn't delete a lot of stuff himself. Some guys who know they are going to off themselves don't want to leave embarrassing porno sites and other stuff for the family to see."

"Emails?"

"Checked his accounts. Lots of nothing. But, again, he could have deleted embarrassing stuff."

"Someone else could also have deleted emails and files. No disrespect, but did your tech guys try to retrieve anything?"

Lin took it well.

"What do you think? This is the C.I.A.? We have good tech people in the department, and when we really need help we can tap the nerds in Silicon Valley. But for an *apparent* suicide? I'd have to get in line. By the time they got around to it, I'd be dead."

I could tell from Lin's inflection on "apparent" that he was frustrated. A possible scream, a too-clean computer and doubts by friends and relatives might not be able to make the S.F.P.D. pull out all the stops, but he wanted to keep the case open.

That meant me. A last resort. But a resort.

"I don't suppose I could see the file, and that computer."

The phone on his desk buzzed.

"I'll get it, Charlie Chan," the cop at the next desk said, and punched a button on his phone.

After identifying himself and listening for a moment, he said, "sure thing" and put the caller on hold.

"It's Vivian," he said to Lin, who punched his own phone.

"Hi, babe," Lin said.

I sat back and politely tuned out what was obviously a domestic conversation, punctuated by laughter, having to do with dinner, homework, a dog, play dates and "the kids".

Lin hung up.

"You and your lady married, Rhode?"

"Working on it," I said, thinking about the ring in the blue box back home. Not to mention the conversation I'd just partially overheard.

"What does that mean?"

"Had to put it on hold."

"Because of this Allender thing?"

"Yeah."

"She holding a torch?"

"No. But she liked the guy. He was apparently a decent sort. Divorce was friendly, as those things go. And she has stayed in touch with his family."

"Solid lady. Want some advice?"

I really didn't, but I needed Lin to like me.

"Sure."

"Don't wait too long. Marriage is great. Viv is the best thing that's ever happened to me. Now, where were we?"

"The file and the computer," I replied.

Lin smiled.

"The computer is back in Allender's apartment."

"I'd like to see it, Inspector. And the rest of the apartment."

Lin reached into one of his desk drawers and came out with an envelope. He shook a key out and handed it to me.

"Noyce told me to cooperate. I don't see the harm, anyway."

"Thanks. What about the file?"

Lin opened another drawer and pulled it out.

"You can't have this. But I'm going to go out for some real coffee. Nice cafe just down the block, next to a Kinkos. Want to join me?"

"Bring me back a latte," the cop at the next desk said. "And an almond croissant."

If a cop in New York squad room said that, he'd be handcuffed. But this was Frisco.

"Another fucking croissant, Wally? You've already got more chins than a Chinese phone book."

We left, with Lin carrying the file. I copied what I needed at the Kinkos while Lin hovered nearby. When I handed the file back to him, I casually said, "By the way, that family video thing on Allender's computer?"

"Yeah. What about it?"

"It was for a surprise party for his sister in Florida. Allender was planning it with their aunt. She said he was gung-ho to be there. For what it's worth, she's absolutely sure he didn't kill himself."

Lin looked at me.

"You son-of-a-bitch."

CHAPTER 14 - STENCILED OUT

I decided to talk to Allender's co-workers before searching his apartment. And I wanted to catch them at work.

Allender & Company was on Clay Street in what is officially called the Financial District in San Francisco, just down the street from a Hilton. There was a homeless man in a cardboard box in the doorway next to the nondescript 10-story building. I was beginning to think there is a local ordinance about it. Every city block has to have at least one homeless person in a doorway or outside a building. Cardboard is mandatory; shopping carts optional.

There was a directory board in the lobby. Dozens of companies, firms and other businesses were listed A to Z, with their room numbers, which I assumed were correlated with their respective floors. The list started with the "B's". There was no "Allender & Company". I checked the listing on my iPhone. I had the right address, 220 Clay Street.

I waited until someone punched a button on one of the elevators. She turned out to be just visiting and didn't know of any company called Allender. The next two elevator people worked in the building but said they never paid much attention to the board. They knew where they were going. I envied them.

I hit pay dirt with the fourth visitor, a delivery boy from a local coffee shop carrying several bags in a large box. Whatever was in the bags smelled very good.

"Yeah, I know Allender," he said. "Only it's not

Allender anymore. I hear the guy died and some other firm took the space over. Actually, that's one of my stops. Three coffees, a bacon and egg on a roll, a croissant and a cinnamon bagel."

He looked at the bills attached to his orders.

"Room 410. They sure didn't wait long. Poor bastard is probably still warm."

"Did you know Allender?"

"Nah. I just leave my stuff with the receptionist."

"What's the name of the new company?"

"Got me. They just gave me the room number. I remember it was Allender from before."

The elevator came and we got on. I got off on the fourth floor. The delivery boy stayed on.

"I work my way down," he said, in case I hadn't figured that out.

A workman was standing outside Room 410, scraping off lettering from the glass door. Only "*pany*" remained to be excised. He opened the door for me. I had to step aside as another workman exited carrying a lamp. When I entered the reception area, I could see other men packing and crating boxes. Two men muscled a large leather couch past me. I heard hammering and ripping.

A young black woman at the reception desk looked up from the magazine she'd been reading. *Vanity Fair.*

"Can I help you," she said.

"I'd like to talk to someone about Kevin Allender."

"Mr. Allender passed away."

She gave me a look that implied she was sad, but not all that broken up about it.

"Yes. I know. I certainly don't want to intrude, but

that's why I'm here. I want to talk to the people he worked with."

"I don't think there is anyone still here. I think they were all let go."

"What about you?"

"Oh, I'm a temp. I'll be gone just as soon as everything is packed away."

"So, you didn't know Mr. Allender."

"No, but I'm sorry he's passed, of course."

"Of course. Would you know how I could reach the old employees?"

"I don't. But maybe Mr. Smith can help you. He's around here someplace. I saw him come in."

"And who might Mr. Smith be?"

"He's just Mr. Smith. In charge of closing up this place. He's the one who hired me to sit here and handle phone calls and visitors."

"Who does he work for?"

"The bank, I guess."

"Bank?"

"Kursk Integrity Bank."

There should be a law against any financial institution using the word "integrity" in their name.

"Can you tell Mr. Smith that I'm here?"

"And you are?"

I was pretty sure that coming across as a private detective might not be the best approach, so I switched gears.

"Miles Archer. Hudson Bay Insurance. We have a policy on Mr. Allender."

The insurance ploy almost invariably works. Insurance means money. Money works.

"Please take a seat," she said, and picked up a phone.

"What seat?"

"Oh, I'm sorry. They already removed them."

I smiled. She smiled, and pretty soon a tall man wearing jeans and a too-small black t-shirt came out of one of the offices.

"I'm Barry Smith," he said, offering his hand.

He was smiling, too. His teeth were yellowish.

"Miles Archer," I said, "Hudson Bay Life."

"Why don't you come back to my office, Mr. Archer."

Smith's office was small and utilitarian, with a dearth of furniture other than a metal desk, a swivel computer chair and one other metal chair, presumably for guests. The walls were unadorned, except for the little doodads used to hang pictures. But what the office lacked in ambiance, it made up for with electronics. Several laptops and a Bloomberg terminal were on the desk, and another laptop on the windowsill behind where Smith sat as he waved me to the other chair.

"You told the girl out front that this has something to do with Allender's insurance?"

"Yes."

I handed him a phony card identifying the phony me and the phony insurance company. I have several such cards, with various companies — insurance, medical, timeshare, charities — whatever gets me in the door. I don't like to use the timeshare card unless I absolutely have to. They all have the same contact numbers and a phony email address. If people bother to call, they get a recorded message. If they email, they get nowhere at all.

As Smith studied the card. I studied him. Tall and thin, with a flat, almost Slavic face. Smallish paunch but otherwise looked like he was in shape. Big across the chest with long, ropey arms. Big nose, which looked like it had been broken more than once, droopy mustache and a very bad and poor-fitting black wig, which didn't quite match the stash or his bushy eyebrows. His eyes were his best feature. Blue and piercing.

"I don't think I've ever heard of Hudson Bay, Mr. Archer."

"We're a very old company. Started out offering policies to fur trappers during the French and Indian Wars. Beaver trade, you know. Made a small fortune on the riders."

"Riders?"

I sighed theatrically, as people do when explaining things to the uninitiated.

"Attachments to policies to cover things outside our control. Such as scalping or being tied to an ant hill. The indigenous tribes were often unfriendly to trappers."

Smith looked stunned.

"Of course, now we primarily offer personal life insurance. Although it seems that the financial world is also very dangerous." I was enjoying myself. "Mr. Allender had a fairly large term policy. With his demise an apparent suicide, we are naturally investigating."

"How large is the policy?"

I shook my head.

"I'm sorry. That's privileged information." I tried to sound officious. "I can tell you that you are not the beneficiary, if that's what you are getting at."

"No. No. I wouldn't expect to be. I hardly knew the man."

"I didn't mean to imply that you and Mr. Allender were, how shall I put it, partners." I gave him a knowing wink. "But this is San Francisco after all."

"I am straight," Smith blurted.

"Well, there is nothing wrong with being gay," I said.

"No, of course not!"

"And it certainly isn't an issue for Allender now, is it? But that's not the reason I'm here. You see there is a two-year suicide exclusion clause on the policy."

"The death was within the two years?"

"Actually, it was right on the cusp, depending on the time zone."

"Time zone?"

"Yes, there is some question whether Pacific Coast Time or Greenwich Mean time applies. There is a nine-hour difference, you know, and, of course, we may have to take into account Daylight Saving."

"You can't be serious, Mr. Archer. You would deny a policy over a few hours' time difference!"

I thought I'd be magnanimous. Smith was so confused he'd probably believe anything I said now. Besides, it wasn't my fictitious money. I leaned in and lowered my voice.

"Just between us, I'm going to recommend we pay off. It's not worth riling up the pet lovers in this country."

"Pet lovers?"

I looked around, as if worried about being heard.

"I'm speaking out of school. I hope I can rely on your discretion. I can't tell you the beneficiary's name, but it does a lot of good work with unwanted dogs and cats. You've probably seen the ads on TV."

"Yes, yes, of course. Very worthy."

"So, you can see how delicate the situation is for us. You know, a company that started out in the fur trade denying a claim that would help puppies and kittens. Do you know what they would do to us on Facebook or Twitter!"

"I can imagine. But I don't see how I can help you."

"Well, you could start by telling me why your bank is obviously liquidating his office. Was Allender in financial trouble? Is this a bankruptcy. A fire sale?"

The questions were obvious, given my "insurance company" interests.

"No. No. He was in good financial shape. And I should know. Our bank financed Allender. We own the lease on this office and basically own all the furniture and equipment."

"Which you are now grabbing. Seems kind of cold. The man isn't dead that long."

Smith shrugged.

"What can I say? Kevin Allender *was* his company. We provided the bricks and mortars. He provided the intellectual capital, so to speak."

"Which means what?"

"Sorry. That's privileged information." He smiled.

"I'm sure you understand."

"What about the people who worked here?"

"What about them?"

"I understand you fired them."

"A couple of clerks. We gave them two weeks' severance. Just business. It's a good job market. They will be fine."

"I'd like to talk to them."

"Why?"

"They knew him. Perhaps they could give me some insight into his state of mind."

"Like I said. They were just clerks."

"I'd still like their names and contact information. Surely, that isn't privileged."

Smith sighed.

"I'll check with our lawyers. If they say it's all right, I'll get the information to you. I have your card. Now, if you will excuse me, I have a lot to do."

I didn't like Barry Smith. There was an air of falseness about him. I couldn't put my finger on it. It was more than his wig and bad teeth. I didn't like his "just clerks" remark or being stonewalled. But since I had lied to get in the door with him, I knew there was nothing else to get. He stood, as did I. He walked me out.

As I left, I heard him angrily tell the temporary receptionist not to bother him again.

CHAPTER 15 - LAPTOP

The laptop was where Lin said it would be, on a black metal work desk in a corner of the kitchen, near a small maple drop-leaf table. There was a single maple chair at the table. Its twin sat next to the computer station. The colors didn't match, but I suspected that Allender, like many men living alone, didn't care.

Before Alice had her say about my digs, I didn't either.

I opened the laptop and was greeted by a red low-battery warning icon. There were only two desk drawers. I found the A/C adapter cord in one of them and plugged in the computer. I knew I could power up the laptop immediately, but it wasn't going anywhere so I decided to search the apartment while the battery restored itself. I hate low batteries.

It was a one-bedroom, one-bath apartment. My search took just over an hour and was cursory. I searched drawers, closets, chests and cabinets. I didn't expect to find much, particularly since somebody had beat me to it. You can always tell when someone has searched a place. It could have been the cops. Lin had mentioned that he'd not found anything suspicious.

I went back into the kitchen and opened the laptop. I'm pretty good with computers. Self-taught, mostly, with a dollop of advanced talent courtesy of Abby, who is a whiz.

So, it didn't take me long to find what I was looking for. Or, rather, to find out that there was nothing worth looking for.

Sure, the computer had some files, word docs, apps, and links, including one to "Dave Hubbard's 90-Second Isometric Workout," a YouTube video that showed a man, presumably Dave, sitting in a chair going through a series of isometrics. I was sitting in a chair but was not inclined to do the exercises just then. But I wrote down the URL for future reference. Nothing wrong with isometrics.

There was another folder, labeled "Anniversary". I opened it. Aunt Maggie had been right. Allender had put together a video presentation for his sister's anniversary celebration incorporating the family photos she'd sent him. It was very well done. Not only had Allender added music, but there were humorous non-family photos and videos, probably taken from various internet and YouTube sites. A couple of the family photos, taken when Allender and his sister were kids in happier times, made my throat constrict.

I made a mental note to make sure Aunt Maggie and Rosemary got the presentation. Maybe there was still time to use it at the party, if it was still on. I had my doubts about that. Photos of a recently dead brother would probably cast a pall over an anniversary celebration. But it wasn't my call. I'd let Aunt Maggie make the decision. She was a tough old bird, with good instincts.

There were some other folders containing banal family information, addresses, phone numbers, birthdays and the like. But nothing worth killing over, or even vaguely business-like. I thought that was strange. It made no sense that there would be nothing related to finance or investing among the files and docs. I would have expected that most people, especially financial types, brought some work home with them.

Of course, Allender might have copied files to a thumb drive, but I hadn't found any during my once-over search. That in itself was weird, unless Allender was so secretive he hid them under the floorboards or behind a light switch. Possible, but not likely. Most people keep their flash drives handy, so they can take them back and forth to work, or whatever. More likely was the possibility that someone wiped the computer and stole the thumb drives. Cops and family might notice a missing computer but might not give a second thought to missing thumb drives.

And Lin didn't mention any thumb drives.

I sat back. It was also unlikely that Allender would have stood still for someone fooling with his computer and stealing his thumb drives. Unless, of course, he was immobilized. There are ways to do that so it will pass muster with a medical examiner, especially after the victim falls 12 stories into a pool.

I knew I was getting ahead of myself. Resigned to do a thorough and dirtier search, I sighed loudly, which you can do in an empty apartment. The one-bedroom now looked like the Chrysler Building to me. I'd have to check the floorboards and unscrew all the damn light switches and fixtures. I'd check all the drains, delve into the toilet tank, stick my hand in everything in the fridge and pantry, melt the ice cubes and generally have a miserable time.

Fortunately, I'd spied some tools in one of the kitchen drawers during my earlier search. As I tried to remember which drawer they were in, I heard someone at the door. Actually, I heard someone picking the lock at the door.

I quickly closed the laptop and moved back into the bathroom. I drew my gun and closed the door, leaving it open just enough to give me a clear view of the rest of the apartment. If it was a casual burglar, he presumably wouldn't start with the bathroom. Of course, if he was a junkie, he might start with the bathroom. In which case, I'd stick my gun under his chin. If he started stealing odds-and-ends elsewhere, I would pop out of my hidey-hole and shout "citizen's arrest!".

I always wanted to do that. But my gut told me it wasn't a junkie or a run-of-the-mill burglar.

The lock-picker was inept, and took so long I thought about just going over to the door and opening it. But while I wanted to know who was breaking into Allender's apartment, I also wanted to know why. And I could only do that by waiting and, hopefully, watching.

Finally, the door opened, and he stepped into the room. Or, rather, she stepped in. It was a little girl, dressed in a black track suit, matching sneakers, a San Francisco Giants baseball cap with an orange logo and a gray San Francisco 49ers backpack with a red logo. Almost color coordinated.

She made a beeline for the computer, unplugged the A/C cord and put everything in her backpack. She turned to leave. The computer had been her target.

I came out of the bathroom, holstering my gun.

"Just a minute, kid," I said.

It didn't have the same ring to it that "citizen's arrest!" would have, but you don't say that to a child.

Except the girl wasn't a child. She couldn't have weighed more than 90 pounds, even with the laptop, and stood only about five feet tall, but she was a grownup, and a pretty one. And as startled as she was, she quickly recovered, darting for the door. I barely beat her to it.

"Take it easy," I said. "We have to talk."

"Listen, snotburger, get out of my way."

Snotburger?

"Why are you so interested in the laptop? There's plenty of other stuff to steal here."

"I have a black belt in Hapkido. Move, or I'll turn you into a pretzel."

I didn't know what Hapkido was, but people who claim to be black belts in something usually aren't. And if they are, I'd bet they never won a brawl. I recalled a time when Maks Kalugin and I were in a Manhattan sports bar when some preppy-looking drunk I'd inadvertently jostled took offense. He was showing off for his buddies. He squared off and assumed the position, hands out, knees bent.

"I know Karate," the poor jerk said. Maks, a drink in his left hand, picked up a bar stool by one of its legs and said, "I know chair", and knocked the guy out cold.

Maks had put down the stool and resumed drinking. He hadn't spilled a drop. The guy's pals gathered him up and left quickly.

"Sure you will," I said now, smiling at the memory. I did like the pretzel line, though. "Now be a good girl and hand over the laptop."

Looking resigned, she held out the backpack.

When I reached for it, she kicked me in the balls.

CHAPTER 16 - ANNA PURNA

I never saw it coming. The kick would have been good from 50 yards out and split the goalposts. It almost split mine. I grunted and immediately assumed the pretzel position. They say that when you are kicked in the family jewels you see stars. It's true. Additionally, I think I saw a few galaxies, a black hole and perhaps a comet.

The girl headed toward the door and almost made it when I managed, between waves of excruciating pain, to pull my gun. I wasn't going to shoot her, but she didn't know that.

I managed to sit upright, my back on the door. She would have to go through me to escape. But now I knew how quick she was, and I wasn't about to take any chances. I was at least twice her size, but the groin kick had leveled the playing field.

"I'll shoot you," I lied, "because I can't do anything else right now."

I think my gasping made my threat sound more ominous. It took all my strength and willpower to hold the gun on her, when all I really wanted to do was roll over and die. A kick in the balls will do that. Of course, I wasn't going to croak, and, if push came to shove, I could work my way past the throbbing agony, which was slowly starting to ebb. I was down to my own solar system.

I waved my gun toward the kitchen table.

"Go sit down," I said. "With your back to the terrace. Put the backpack on the table."

I was proud of myself. No gasps. I slowly got to

my feet as she sat. I locked the door and gingerly walked over to the table and sat opposite her. I tried not to grimace as I eased on to the chair. I don't think I succeeded. She looked pleased.

"You weren't going to shoot me, were you? If you weren't leaning on the door, I would have made it."

"Probably. Why don't you try now?"

She shrugged.

"I've lost the element of surprise. You don't look like the kind of man who would be caught off guard twice. Even by a girl."

"What the hell is Hapkido?"

"A Korean variant of Karate that stresses punches, kicks, throws and joint locks."

"You must have aced the class that dealt with kicks."

She actually smiled.

"That wasn't Hapkido. I learned it in a self-defense class at the Y."

"What's your name?"

She looked at me and shook her head. I reached into the backpack and took out the laptop. And her wallet, which I opened.

Her driver's license identified her as Annalise Purna. She looked a lot like her license photo, which surprised me. My I.D. photo looks like I should be holding a numbered plaque in a police station. There were credit cards, including a black American Express Card, with her name on them. The wallet also contained five one-hundred-dollar bills. If Annalise was a burglar, she'd done quite well for herself. I looked up. She shrugged.

"Now that you know who I am," she said, "who the fuck are you?"

"I'm the Potty Mouth Inspector."

"What, are you my mother?"

"I'm a guy who belongs in this apartment, courtesy of the San Francisco Police Department."

"You a cop?"

"Private."

If she was impressed, she didn't show it.

"Why is a private investigator in Kevin's apartment?"

I love it when someone I'm questioning starts asking me questions. Especially when that someone had recently tried to geld me. But I was intrigued by her casual demeanor and the fact that she apparently knew Allender.

"I work for his family," I answered.

It was true, sort of.

"Do they also think he was murdered?"

"Do you?" I said, carefully.

She slapped a hand on the table. Remembering the kick, I almost jumped. I knew I wasn't dealing with Tinker Bell.

"Of course, I do," she exclaimed. "Why the fuck do you think I'm here?" She paused. "Sorry."

"I thought you were here to steal Allender's computer."

"It's my damn computer now. 'Damn' is OK, right?"

Her voice dripped with sarcasm.

"Nobody likes a wise ass," I said.

She smiled.

"Anyway, I bought it for him and showed him all its bells and whistles."

Suddenly, she got coy.

"You have anything to prove who you say you are?"

I took out my wallet and passed it to her. She studied my private investigator's license.

"You work in New York?"

"Yes."

"Why is a New York private eye out here?"

She seemed genuinely interested. I told her.

"Wow," she said. "Your girlfriend. That's romantic. I didn't know Kev was married. Got a picture of his ex?"

"In the wallet."

She rooted around and quickly found a photo of Alice I took at a Kentucky Derby party in Staten Island the previous year. I'm not very talented with my iPhone camera but I'd gotten lucky, so I had it printed. It was my favorite. Alice was dressed to the nines and looked a 10, maybe an 11.

"Wow. She's gorgeous. What's her name?"

"Alice."

"You should marry her."

I took my wallet back.

"Can we get back to why you want the computer? There is nothing on the computer that seems important."

She rolled her eyes, reached for the laptop and opened it. Her fingers flew around the computer, almost faster than I could track. It gave me a chance to size her up. Small face, sharp features nicely proportioned, wide eyes, black hair cut short sticking out from her cap. I couldn't decide if she looked like Anna Kendrick or Kate Mara. Either way, Annalise Purna was pixie attractive. She tucked her left leg up on the chair as she worked. There was a small tattoo of a Koala Bear on her ankle. It was a nice ankle. I suspected her legs were also very nice. She was small-breasted, but I also suspected they would pass muster. I'm monogamous by choice, but I remember an old priest praising a woman's looks who told me that just because someone was on a diet didn't mean one couldn't look at the menu.

"That's funny," she said after about two minutes. "You are right. It's been wiped."

"You're sure?"

"Of course, I'm sure. All of our work is missing. Someone probably copied it to a flash drive and then deleted it."

"What about Kevin's flash drives? I was about to tear the place apart when you distracted me by breaking in."

"Waste of time. Kevin didn't use flash drives for business. Was always misplacing them. He'd store bits and pieces of his algorithms and calculations and stuff in the cloud, but individually none of it would make sense to anyone but him. Even I would have a hard time figuring how to put all of it together. His main ideas were on his laptop. Whoever wiped it should have taken it, too. I guess they thought that would make the cops suspicious or something, if the computer disappeared. But, no matter. The info is still on this laptop."

"What do you mean it's still on this laptop?"

Annalise Purna smiled.

"I told you this was my computer, too. I installed all sorts of back doors and secret files that only I can access. Every time they deleted something, a copy automatically went onto the hard drive, disguised as a systems app or a game file. You know, like Solitaire or Hearts. I have the key to unlock those apps and files. It will take some time, but I can retrieve it all."

"How do you know they didn't figure out your back doors, or whatever you call them?"

She gave me the same look that Sister Rose gave me in my elementary-school math class when I asked a dumb question.

"What do you think I was just doing. Typing my résumé? I just checked. They are good, but I'm about the best there is."

"It seems as if you've decided to trust me all of a sudden. Just because I flash a license. If I was a bad guy, you'd be dead."

She laughed and turned the laptop around so that I could see the screen. In separate windows there was my photo, some news stories about me, my Facebook and other social media pages, phone numbers, address, and just about anything else that was public record. And some things that probably shouldn't be.

Jesus Christ.

"You researched me while we were talking," I said. "I thought you were checking computer files."

"That only took a few seconds, Mr. Rhode. Not a very common name. Alton Rhode. Funny name."

"You should talk."

"My father thought I would rise to great heights," she said. "He always called me Anna. Most people do."

It hit me. The name of the world's second-tallest mountain.

"Anna Purna."

"Cool, huh?"

I had to admit it was.

"Were you and Allender an item?"

She shook her head.

"No. Not yet, anyway. We were too excited just working on our project."

She looked pensive,

"But lately I began to feel something, and I think he did, too. I think we were on the verge. Who knows?"

She paused, and I thought I saw her eyes glisten.

"Now I'll never know. Anyway, this isn't all business for me. Like you, it's personal."

"Sorry, Anna."

"Sure. I just know Kevin would never kill himself."

"So, you think whoever wiped his computer murdered him?

"That's the thing. There wasn't anything on it worth killing for. I wanted the laptop because I knew Kevin did stuff at home and I didn't want to wait to get my hands on it. Our project needs some tweaking. I didn't want to lose precious time convincing the cops or the family or the courts to give me the computer. With my luck, someone would just steal it."

"You mean, someone else besides you."

"Whatever."

"Anna, this makes no sense. Why kill someone and wipe his computer if there was nothing on it worth killing for?"

"Hey. You're the detective. You figure it out."

"It might help if I knew what was wiped. Just what were the two of you working on."

"Explaining it will take some time. I'd rather not stick around here if it's all the same to you. Some real cops might show up."

"That's not a problem. I have permission to be here."

"Do you have permission to steal this laptop? Let's go to my place."

CHAPTER 17 - CAVALLO POINT

"Sorry about the kick in the balls," she said. "Does it still hurt?"

I was probably walking a bit funny when we left the building.

"I've heard it's a bitch. Like child birth or a kidney stone."

Women always say that. If they felt the way I did after the kick every time they had a baby, the human race would have died out long ago.

"Let's change the subject," I said.

"Sure. But I guess I should thank you for not shooting me."

"The day is still young, sweetheart."

I got out my smart phone.

"What are you doing?"

"I don't have a car," I said. "I've been using Uber to get around."

"Put it away. We'll take my ride."

With that, she reached to her pocket and pulled out a small remote and walked a few yards to a brand-new gray-and-silver Lexus SUV. On its side it said, "Cavallo Point Resort". I saw the parking lights flash and heard the car doors click open. She climbed in on the driver's side.

"Well, what are you waiting for," she said. "Get in."

I was suspicious. My relationship with the local gendarmes wasn't all that solid. We had a "stolen" laptop in our possession. And I recalled Anna's black Amex card and all the cash. She was a computer genius. How hard would it be to dummy I.D.s up? And, of course, I knew she wasn't above a little burglary.

"Where did you get this car?"

She laughed.

"Don't worry. It's not stolen. I work at Cavallo Point. As a tech consultant. It's a Lexus Partner Property. We have a bunch of these. I get to use one whenever I need it."

I still hesitated.

"Don't be such a worry wart," she said. "Look in the glove compartment if you don't believe me."

I got in and did. There was a folder containing the car's registration and proof of insurance, as well a small laminated card with a "Cavallo Point Resort" logo and her picture, identifying "Dr. Annalise Purna" as a "Technical Consultant". I looked at her.

"Doctor?"

"Ph.D.'s in Computer Science and Nano Technology at Stanford."

"Alice teaches at Barnard."

I didn't know why I said that. Annalise had started out being what I thought was a runty little kid. Now I was trying to impress her. I wasn't even sure what 'Nano Technology' was.

"So, you're not a run-of-the-mill burglar."

She smiled.

"I'm not a run-of-the-mill anything. Can I curse now, when it's appropriate?"

"Sure, Doc."

"Fuckin' A! Where are you staying, Alton?"

"The Westin St. Francis at Union Square."

"Fatty Arbuckle's crib."

"Fatty Arbuckle?"

"Silent Screen comedy star who allegedly raped and killed a girl there. He was acquitted, but the studio's blacklisted him and ruined his career."

"You're a movie buff?"

"I'm an everything buff. Anyway, the St. Francis is a great place. But not cheap. I can save you some serious dough at Cavallo. How does a hundred bucks a night sound? Place usually goes for three times that. But I get a room for free as part of my deal and they give me a humongous break on other rooms for family. I'll tell them you're my uncle."

"Thanks a lot."

She laughed,

"Put on your seat belt, Unc."

I did, and was soon glad.

Annalise Purna obviously knew San Francisco. She drove like Steve McQueen in *Bullitt*. It made me long for a bad-weather plane landing. The knuckles on my hands, which were on my knees, were again white. I relaxed them and tried to act calm, not easy to do when one is occasionally weightless plunging down one of the city's vertiginous streets.

She pushed a button on the CD player and the car filled with a thundering bass sound with a hypnotic beat. If I closed my eyes, as I was sorely tempted to do, I could have imagined myself on starship.

"Like it?" she asked. "It's *Radioactive,* by *Imagine Dragons.*"

"Catchy. Listen, should I survive this ride, I may be in town longer than I thought. I have to buy some clothes."

"Will a Walmart Superstore do?"

"If it doesn't, I'd be pretty hard to please."

A Walmart Superstore is where things you don't really need go to die. I sometimes lose myself in the aisles.

This time, however, I managed to buy only just enough basic traveling clothes to keep me going for a while.

An hour later, my Walmart packages were in the back seat of the Lexus. I envied them as Anna resumed light speed. But after a brief run we screeched to a halt outside the Westin St. Francis. The doorman opened the car door for me and didn't ask Anna to move, probably because he saw the Cavallo Point logo. Professional courtesy.

I went to my room, repacked my carry-on luggage and checked out. It was close to check-out time, so the hotel only charged me for one night.

After leaving the hotel, we were mercifully slowed by traffic and various lights on the road leading to the Golden Gate Bridge. The famous span, with its view of the city and surrounding hills, not to mention Alcatraz, always impresses me. Even Annalise drove across the bridge at a respectable pace, and pointed out some sights, although I could barely hear her over *Imagine Dragons*. But as soon as we exited the bridge and passed the cutoff to Sausalito, she resumed warp speed, twisting and turning on a winding two-lane that offered both magnificent views and the possibility of a fatal plunge.

Annalise hit another button on the CD player.

"This is probably more your speed, Mr. Rhode. *Duran Duran.* They made it for the James Bond movie filmed here. *A View to a Kill.* Roger Moore played 007. I didn't think he was a great Bond, but that's one of his best."

I knew the song. It was catchy, and also heart-pounding. She started singing:

Dance into the fire
That fatal kiss is all we need
Dance into the fire
To fatal sounds of broken dreams
Dance into the fire
That fatal kiss is all we need
Dance into the fire
When all we see is the view to a kill.

"Very appropriate," I murmured, looking down the hillside.

We took another turn at warp speed. A canyon beckoned. We made it and we again slowed behind a trolley-like bus full of sightseers. We came to a fork in the road. A sign pointed toward "Fort Baker" and "Cavallo Point" to the right. The bus went left.

"I wonder what Yogi would do," Anna said.

We went to the right down a hill, passed several barracks-looking buildings and pulled in front of two large wooden Victorian structures with verandas, on which dozens of people, some with kids, sat eating at long tables or rocking in chairs. Across a broad expanse of lawn, one could see the top of the Golden Gate Bridge sticking up over the hills. Everything sat in kind of a huge natural amphitheater flanked by more "barracks" and three-story Victorian homes. Annalise parked in a row of identical Lexus SUVs. I looked around.

"I know I've never been here," I said. "But this looks awfully familiar."

"The news shows shoot a lot of their interviews on the lawn. With the bridge in the background. *Sunday Morning*, with Jane Pauley, was just out here. Not her, one of her correspondents."

"Where's the fort?"

"This is it. This whole area was the site of Fort Baker. The Cavallo Point people leases all this land and the buildings, most of which are old barracks and officer housing. There is still a military museum that houses artifacts. Very popular with the kiddies. And you can run across the occasional old cannon. It's all part of the Golden Gate National Recreation Area. On the other side of the bridge is Fort Point. The two bases commanded the entrance to the harbor."

Anna smiled.

"I'm a military buff, too."

We went into what turned out to be Cavallo Point's administration building. An attractive young Asian woman behind the reception desk greeted Anna with kisses on both cheeks.

"This is Sandy Wong," Anna said. "My best friend here. I don't have that many friends, so she's probably my best friend anywhere. Sandy, this is my uncle Alton. Can he have a room near me?"

Sandy Wong smiled indulgently. I suspected that Anna had several "uncles".

Anna walked over to another desk to say hello to some of the other staff.

"Anna takes a lot of getting used to," Sandy Wong said. "But she's worth it. Welcome to Cavallo Point, the Lodge at the Golden Gate."

After I checked in, Anna and I drove up to our rooms.

CHAPTER 18 - REVELATIONS

A steep winding road led up to a building housing a group of condo apartments about a quarter mile up the hill from the main lodge and administration building. The condos were modern and were obviously added to the Cavallo Point complex after Fort Baker ceased to be a military installation. Anna parked next to the building, in a spot that had the word "Reserved" painted on it.

"Another perk," she said. "Most of the parking spots are empty anyway this time of the year, and I rarely use mine, but it's nice to have it. A girl likes to feel special, you know."

Anna walked me to my apartment and got me settled in.

"My room is just two doors down, next to my parking spot," she said.

We agreed to have dinner at the resort restaurant at 7 PM. She said she would take care of the reservation.

"Come by my place at 6:45," she said. "We can walk down to the restaurant. It's one of the best in the Bay Area. But I'm beat now. I need a few hours' sleep. I'll tell you everything I know at dinner."

After she left, I changed into the jogging clothes I'd bought. I had almost two hours to kill and if I took a nap, which I needed, I'd feel miserable. I longed for my own running shoes, but the runners I purchased in Walmart looked comfortable enough. I'd take it easy until they were broken in.

I used a small map of Fort Baker and Cavallo Point that was in my room to orient myself and then set out.

There were an interlocking set of paths for hiking, biking and jogging that wound through and around the complex. I estimated that if I used them all I'd get five miles in. I kept a slow but steady pace, using my new jogging shoes as an excuse, although in reality the often- hilly terrain and my burning calf muscles had more to do with it.

Despite the chill, I soon worked up a sweat. I ran past a chapel, the administration buildings, around the huge parade ground, a Coast Guard Station, a children's museum and finally a fishing pier that jutted into San Francisco Bay. I headed back along a trail that ran parallel to a highway in the hills above the complex. By the time I reached my condo, I felt pretty good. Though I was glad to stop.

I showered, shaved and dressed. My tan L.L. Bean travel blazer passed muster and I looked in the mirror to make sure my gun did not show in its shoulder holster. I knocked on Anna's door at exactly 6:45 PM. When she opened the door, I was momentarily taken aback. She was wearing a black short-sleeve lace sheath dress, with pearl earrings and a simple pearl necklace. Her hair was down and framed her face. High heel peep-toe mesh pumps made her a bit taller and accented what I already knew were toned calves.

"Ta-da," she said, and twirled. "How do I look?"

"What have you done with Anna?"

She laughed.

"I bet you didn't expect a computer nerd like me to dress up, did you?"

"Anna, you look fabulous. The most beautiful burglar I've ever come across."

"That's Dr. Burglar to you," she said.

She put her arm through mine as she shut the door. I caught a lingering waft of a bittersweet smell I recognized.

"Let's walk down to the restaurant. This is the first night I feel I can relax since Kevin died."

Anna was indeed relaxed, having obviously just smoked some grass. That was fine by me. I wanted her talkative. And I got an earful on the way down to the restaurant.

"Fort Baker is comprised of 335 acres and was originally inhabited by the Coast Mohawk tribe," she said. "But they were displaced by European settlers, starting in 1775 when the *San Carlos*, a Spanish vessel, entered San Francisco Bay. After the Mexican-American War, private speculators grabbed the land, but in 1866 the U.S. Government took everything over and made a fort, installing cannons to protect the harbor. By the way, the fort is named after Edward Dickenson Baker, an Oregon Senator who got himself killed in the Civil War. He's buried at the Presidio. I wish more Senators went to war now, don't you? Anyway, Fort Baker was active in one way or another right through the Cold War. Now it's a national park and the habitat for many animal species, including the mission blue butterfly, which is endangered. They must be, because I've only seen them once or twice."

The remainder of the walk was punctuated by various stops at historic sites, some of which I'd passed on my run earlier. Finally, we reached the main lodge.

"Let's have a drink at the Farley bar," Anna said.

She approached the hostess standing at a podium in the hallway.

"Mary, can you save us that table I like in the back? Say, for 7:45?"

"Sure, Anna."

The tavern was to the left of the hostess stand and turned out to be a charming spot, its bar carved from a fallen tree and its seats made of cozy leather.

"It's named after Farley, the comic strip character in the Chronicle," Anna intoned, continuing her marijuana-enthused travelogue.

The bartender greeted her warmly.

"I'll have a Third Degree, straight up," Anna ordered.

She turned to me.

"Appropriate, don't you think, since you want to grill me."

The "Third Degree" cocktail turned out to be a gin martini with absinthe added for an additional kick. I also had a martini, sans the absinthe.

The drink seemed to slow Anna's patter down a bit, and her visage took on a dreamy look. Maybe it was the absinthe.

I knew something about absinthe. Enough to avoid it. It's a potent anise-based spirit, also known as "the green fairy", that was banned in the U.S. until 2007, presumably because it had hallucinogenic effects on imbibers. I read somewhere that absinthe's power came mostly from its high alcohol content, but looking at Anna's dreamy gaze, which was directed at me, I was not so sure. I'd have to be careful with her. Marijuana, gin and absinthe probably made for an interesting evening.

We chatted for a while with the bartender, a San Francisco 49ers fan only too happy to point out the failings of my New York Giants and to rub it in about the Jets. But he made a hell of a cocktail. When I tried to pay, he just shook his head.

"They comp my drinks," Anna said. "I have to go wee-wee. I'll meet you at the hostess stand."

As she walked to the rest room, two men at the bar stared after her. Then, they looked at each other and smiled. On the surface it appeared to be a typical male reaction to a pretty woman. But there was something about the pair that was off, almost comical. They were dressed in almost identical dark green suits. Only their ties were different, although neither tie went with green. And neither suit fit very well. One of the men was much taller than the other. Both had spiky black uncombed hair and thick black eyebrows.

They reminded me of Bert and Ernie on the Muppets. I turned to the bartender.

"Is the circus in town?"

"Huh?"

"Never mind."

I left a twenty on the bar and departed. I chatted with Mary, the hostess, for a minute. Then Anna joined us, and Mary summoned a waiter to bring us to a quiet table in the adjacent Murray Circle restaurant by a window with a twilight view of the Golden Gate.

"Dinner is on me," she said. "I have an expense account here."

"Just what do you do for these people?"

"Like I told you. I consult. Their computer billing

was a total shambles. And their inventory control, maintenance and employee compensation systems would have benefited from an abacus, let alone my expertise. Hell, I saved them a million in taxes alone. I get 20 percent of everything I save them, plus perks."

A waiter appeared and passed out menus. He recited a few specials, many of which included the word "organic."

"I'm the local," Anna said. "Why don't you let me order?"

"You're the doctor," I said, fingers crossed.

Anna was so thin and healthy looking, I feared I was headed for a lot of legumes and sprouts.

I needn't have worried.

"We'll have a dozen and a half Puget Sound oysters. Six Kumamotos, six Olympias and six Little Skookums."

"I'm sorry, but we're out of Olympias. How about the Miradas? Just got some in."

"Sure. I love them, too. Then, Caesar salads and New York strip steaks, medium rare, with baked potatoes."

She looked at me.

"Fine," I said, relieved.

"Champagne?"

I nodded. She picked up the wine list.

"And a bottle of Billecart-Salmon Brut Reserve."

The waiter left.

"OK, you can start your third degree, Alton."

I laughed.

"Why don't you just tell me what you and Kevin Allender were working on together."

CHAPTER 19 - BLOCKCHAINS

"What do you know about blockchains?"

"Something to do with cryptocurrency, right? Like Bitcoin."

Anna smiled. I sensed a lecture coming on.

"Blockchains are the architecture, if you will, on which Bitcoin and other cryptocurrencies are built. Without a blockchain there is no Bitcoin or any other crypto. Just like without the internet there is no email."

"Perhaps you should back up. Just what is a blockchain?"

"At its core, a blockchain isn't much different from any other database. It stores information. But not in one spot. The information is stored on computers all over the world. It is decentralized."

"And that's good?"

"It's great! It's revolutionary."

"Why? Doesn't that complicate things?"

"Would you be happier if all your information, or the information Google or Yahoo or whoever has on you, was stored in one place, where it could be blown up, or hit by an earthquake or a tsunami?"

"There is backup."

"Of course, but whatever is centralized can't only be damaged, it can be manipulated."

"Hacked?"

"Hacked. Spammed. Erased. Changed. Whatever."

The waiter brought our champagne, poured us two flutes and put the bottle in an ice bucket next to the table. Anna and I clinked glasses and drank.

"Excellent," I said.

"My favorite," she replied. "Anyway, decentralization means that none of that can happen because if the information is stored on computers all over the world, no one person, or country, or entity can screw around with it."

"But if everyone has the information, where is the security?"

The oysters came, on a big platter with ice, and three dipping sauces in little bowls. I recognized two of the dips.

"What's that one," I said, pointing at a greenish sauce.

"Lime and garlic," Anna said. "Try it."

I did. It was good, but I preferred the red seafood sauce and horseradish. The oysters themselves were excellent. They were cold and tasted like the ocean.

"It must have been a brave man, or woman, who ate the first oyster," Anna said, expertly slurping one. "Considering that they look like phlegm on a shell."

"Thanks for that."

"Sorry. But where was I?"

"If everyone has the information, where is the security?"

"Because no one knows what they have. And if they don't know what they have, how can they, or anyone, fuck with it?"

"Why don't they know what they have?"

Anna pursed her lips.

"You know, I'm probably explaining this wrong."

"Don't sweat it. If you explained it right, I probably still wouldn't get it."

"OK. Instead of the word 'information', which

implies something people can read or understand, substitute 'data', as in a group of numbers. This data is stored in groups, called blocks. Each block is time stamped, given its own numerical hashtag and linked to one block created just before it in time. Thus, there is a line of blocks. A chain of blocks."

"A blockchain."

"Give that man another oyster."

I felt like I had just passed algebra in Sister Mary Marmalade's class.

"Now," Anna continued, "each block has three bits of crucial information. The time data on transmission, the block's own unique hash and the hash of the previous block."

"Back up. Go over the hash thing again."

"We call it a 'nonce', or number used only once. It's like a fingerprint, a numerical fingerprint, a unique string of numbers automatically calculated based on the information, or data if you will, stored on the block. If you change one of the numbers, you not only change that block's identity, but the previous block's, and the block before that and so on. The entire chain is compromised. Now, it's theoretically possible to find the random numbers on a single block. Today's super computers can do it in a few minutes. But that's one block on a single copy of a ledger, say the Bitcoin ledger. But there are thousands of copies of that ledger spread around the world. Before I wanted to manipulate Bitcoin, say to transfer the electronic coins into an account or convert them into fiat, or real currency like dollars, I'd have to gain control of thousands of computers and repeat the whole process on each one."

She slurped another bivalve.

"It's not only practically impossible, but the rest of the network would notice if I tried. No single party has control over what data goes on a block. Exact copies are stored on thousands of computers. Information can be added to a blockchain but blocks can't be edited, the new info can't contradict previous data and everyone on the network is keeping an eye on it. It's fraud proof."

Our Caesar salads came.

"You going to eat your anchovies?" Anna asked.

"Yes."

She stuck her tongue out at me.

"Anna, you said blockchains are fraud proof. What about Silk Road?"

"I thought you didn't know anything about blockchains."

"Everyone in law enforcement has heard of Silk Road. That's where I heard the term cryptocurrency. But that was the extent of my knowledge, until now. You'd make a hell of a teacher, kid."

"Thanks."

I gave her two of my anchovies.

"Teacher's pet," she said. "Anyway, Silk Road was a drug scandal right here in Frisco, back in 2011. Guy set up a trafficking scheme that used cryptocurrencies to finance it, pay off dealers and launder fiat currencies. He was caught and sent away for life. But he didn't manipulate the blockchain, just used Bitcoin for his own purposes, figuring he could get around regular banking regulators, which he did for a while. It was a brilliant idea but basically it was just a drug deal that unraveled. He used the system, he didn't game it."

Our steaks came. While we ate, and finished the champagne, I asked Anna to go over everything again. She did, and I finally got it, or at least as much of it as I was ever going to get. When we finished, she said she didn't want dessert but wouldn't mind having an after-dinner drink back in the Farley bar.

"Only if you let me buy," I said. "And how about if you let me leave a tip here. I'm beginning to feel like a kept man."

"Maybe later," she said with a mischievous smile. "But for now, I'll let you be gallant."

***

The Farley was now hopping. I looked for the two men whose gazes had seemed to follow Anna when she went to the ladies' room earlier. Bert and Ernie had apparently left.

Sandy Wong was sitting at a high-top table with a handsome Asian man and called over to us. We joined them. Sandy introduced her companion, whose name was Jian Chen.

"Jian is the Assistant Cultural Attaché for the Chinese consulate in San Francisco," Sandy said, proudly.

Chen was tall for a Chinese. He was very good-looking, with slicked-back jet-black hair and high cheekbones. He was wearing a charcoal gray suit, white shirt and a maroon tie. He had a powerful handshake and looked like he worked out. His smile was quick and seemed genuine. He insisted on buying us a round of drinks.

I had a Maker's Mark bourbon in a snifter and Anna had absinthe on the rocks. All the booze was beginning to get to me. I couldn't imagine what it was doing to Anna. Still, we had a very nice time. Chen spoke perfect English and knew a lot about American baseball and we hit it off.

It turned out that he was the same age as I and had been in the diplomatic service for almost a decade, with postings all over the United States. I presume his facility with the language came in very handy. I caught snippets of Anna and Sandy's conversation. They apparently made plans to meet for an early breakfast. Chen and I both smiled at that.

"Ah, youth," I said. "It's wasted on the young."

Chen laughed.

"There is an old Chinese proverb," he said. "Youth misspent is not wasted."

We clinked glasses on that.

"What about you, Alton, if I may call you Alton. What do you do?"

I told him. He made no comment and I found it a bit strange that he didn't ask why I was in San Francisco. But then I remembered he was a diplomat. Perhaps they are trained not to be too overly nosy.

Mary, the restaurant hostess, came over to us.

"Sandy, your table is ready."

The couple got up to leave. As we said our goodbyes, Sandy said, "Oh, by the way, Anna, someone was asking for you at the desk."

"Who was it?"

"Said his name was Smith. Thought he was being

coy at first, but he sounded legit. Said he knew you."

"Barry Smith?"

"Yeah. That's him."

"Did he say what he wanted?"

"No. But he said he had to see you in person. Said he would stop by in the morning if you were staying over. I said you were. Was that OK? I didn't tell him where you lived, and he didn't ask."

"It's fine. Barry knows where my condo is. He's been there. Probably something to do with what I'm working on with Kursk. He's a bit of a worry-wart. See you at breakfast."

"Don't forget the keys, Anna."

"I won't."

Sandy and Chen left.

"Keys?"

"Sandy is going into town early," Anna said. "She forgot to arrange a car and the Lexus guy won't be in until 9 AM or so. So, she's going to borrow my car. We always meet for an early breakfast when we're here together. Don't worry, I'll bring you back something. You can sleep in."

She smiled enigmatically.

"You may need the rest."

I wondered what she meant by that.

"I didn't know you knew Barry Smith," I said.

I'd told her that I'd stopped by Allender's firm.

"Sure. His bank was going to help fund the bitcoin mining for Golden Gate, and then act as the financial conduit until we became autonomous. For a fee, of course. Sometimes he came by to see how Kevin and I were progressing. He's a big deal at Kursk. But like I said, he's a worry wart."

"Back up, Anna. What's Golden Gate?"

"It's the not-for-profit Kevin and I were planning to set up using our proprietary blockchain."

"When I spoke to him, he was in the process of dismantling Allender's office."

"I guess that's just business," she said. "Life goes on. It sucks, but there it is. I'm surprised a bit. He and Kevin seemed to get along. They even went fishing and did other guy things together."

Smith hadn't mentioned anything to me about blockchains. But then, why should he. I was just an insurance guy to him.

But he also said he hardly knew Kevin Allender. And that was an out-and-out lie.

"Listen," Anna said. "Let's blow this place."

She looked around.

"Too many ears. Let's go back to my condo and I'll explain Golden Gate to you."

CHAPTER 20 - GOLDEN GATE

Anna took my arm as we walked up the hill. She seemed slightly tipsy.

"You know what they say," she said. "Absinthe makes the heart grow fonder."

"That's terrible," I said, but filed the pun away for the future.

I wasn't feeling bad myself. The night air was cool but refreshing.

Once in her condo, Anna excused herself and went into her bedroom. When she came out, she was barefoot and smoking a joint. Without her shoes, she barely came up to my shoulders. She had another joint in her other hand.

"Want one of these?"

I shook my head.

"Tell me about Golden Gate."

I wanted to get as much information as I could before the gin, absinthe and grass took its toll, although I had to say she seemed to have it all together for such a small girl. I felt my age. Anna shrugged and sat on the couch, uncurled her legs and rested her bare feet on my lap.

"Do you mind?"

"As long as you don't kick me again." I said. "They're fine."

The sharp, sweet smell of marijuana soon permeated the room. She leaned back against a cushion and smiled slyly.

"Golden Gate," I prompted, and tweaked a toe.

Anna looked slightly annoyed.

"Oh, well. Golden Gate is the name of a system we developed. A system where socially conscious or charitable organizations, non-profits and NGOs can inhabit a non-partisan crypto-based universe with corporate America."

"What's an NGO?"

"Non-Governmental Organization. Like the Red Cross, or the Wildlife Fund. We're going to mine cryptocurrencies and then use the bitcoins created to compensate people who actively try to save the planet. They, in turn, can use their bitcoins to pay for environmentally safe goods. Say, you volunteer for Habitat for Humanity. Or clean up a beach. We give you one of our bitcoins. You accumulate bitcoins, which you then could spend to buy groceries. A big grocery chain would jump at the opportunity to look like its helping people or the environment. Or, because speculators realize that bitcoins now have intrinsic worth, they bid their price up. So, even if you didn't spend your bitcoins on groceries, or gas, or a vacation, whatever, you have a growing investment."

She took a hit on her joint.

"Of course, until we recruit enough companies or socially committed organizations to accept cryptocurrencies, we will give people the option to turn their bitcoins into fiat currencies they can use to buy stuff. We may also allow them to convert their electronic coins into precious metals. It's quite simple, really."

"Anna, let's get one thing straight. Nothing you are explaining is simple to a normal human. Try to speak some plain English. I'm a pretty smart guy, but if I'm going to figure out what the hell is going on, try to imagine that I'm an earthling."

She laughed.

"Sorry."

She took a puff on her weed and then held it out for me.

"Again, no thanks. I can't understand you now."

She let out the fragrant smoke.

"OK. I'll dumb it down."

"Thanks. I think."

"Cryptocurrencies, bitcoins, or whatever you want to call them, only exist as electronics bytes in computers. Their sole purpose is to exist. When they start out, they aren't backed by anything solid, such as gold or even paper, or fiat, currencies like dollars. Of course, the dollar isn't backed by anything anymore. Its value is based on the so-called full faith and credit of the United States. As long as we're top dog, militarily, financially and so on, people can rely on it. And the dollar forms the basis for other national currencies, some of which also have their own backing, like precious metals. Now, a lot of very smart people think the whole structure is a house of cards. And recent financial catastrophes that have shaken the world financial system enforce their suspicions. Follow me so far?"

I nodded. Anna's transformation from a hard-drinking pothead to financial expert was surreal. Then I remembered she had two doctorates. I felt like taking notes.

"Anyway, some of these smart people decided that they needed alternative ways of paying for things, ways not tied to existing banks and Governments they didn't trust. So, they used blockchain technology to create cryptocurrencies. Or vice versa. It's a chicken or the egg kind of thing. I don't think anyone knows. Point is, if you have enough money, as in real money, to mine bitcoins, you can create a closed financial universe, or circle, if you like, in which people can buy and sell bitcoins, or use them to buy real things. All without involving third parties, or middlemen, like banks."

"You keep talking about mining bitcoins. I'm a little hazy on that. What exactly is 'mining'."

Anna wiggled her toes. They were painted red.

"Don't I have nice toes?"

"Terrific. World class. What's mining?"

"Well, bitcoins don't just come out of thin air. I mean, they are even less than thin air when you come right down to it. Just bytes of information. But they have to be created. Each byte, or bit, has lots of data, bits of information, on it that makes it unique. I mean, if they were all the same, they wouldn't be worth anything, right? The beauty of blockchains is that it is virtually impossible to break into any blockchain because each bitcoin has a unique set of data attached to it. I already told you that."

I was beginning to understand, though not to the point I could explain it to someone else.

"Creating millions and billions of the unique bytes in a blockchain takes computer power. Lots of computer power. Computers are costly. And computers run on electricity, which is very costly. The people who create the blockchain bytes are called miners. But instead of, say, coal or diamonds, they are 'mining' cryptocurrency bitcoins."

"And you and Allender had the financing to mine your bitcoins?"

Anna laughed.

"Hell, no! That's why we partnered with Kursk."

"Barry Smith?"

"Yes. Barry was going to provide the money to create our bitcoins."

"What would Barry get out of it?"

"Well, his bank, Kursk, would handle initial transactions and provide a way for investors and speculators to turn their bitcoins into fiat currencies or gold if they wanted. For a fee, of course."

"Assuming they were worth something and there was a market to trade them, right?"

"Hey, you're paying attention."

"I have my moments. But let me ask you something. The blockchain you plan to create may have unique bitcoins. But the idea isn't unique. What's to prevent someone else with more money from cannibalizing Golden Gate? Or aren't you worried about competition?"

"We hoped someone copied our idea! We wanted a lot of people to create socially conscious cryptocurrencies. It's not like we all wouldn't make out well. Competitors would be smart to just license our product, rather than mine their own. But the more the merrier. The idea is to save the planet and improve lives. Kevin was adamant about that, and so am I. Barry thought we should patent the idea, but Kevin scotched that right away."

"How did Barry take it?"

"Actually, he surprised me. I mean, he went through the motions. We were giving up a lot of money, blah, blah, blah. But he didn't put up many objections when we dug our heels in. He's just a banker, after all. Those guys make their living on fees. I read somewhere that U.S. banks pocketed something like $40 billion on overdraft fees alone. What a racket. No wonder people want their own currencies. I'm not sure Barry got the whole idea, anyway. He's not a bad guy. A bit of a creep with that wig and all, but Kevin got along with him. I don't like wigs on men. Unless, they are dying or something. I like my men au natural."

"One thing still confuses me, Anna. Kursk is a bank. I thought the whole idea was to eliminate the need for banks."

"It is, silly. But startups still need traditional financing systems to get going. And I don't think we will ever get to a time when regular national currencies disappear. At least while there are still nations. Look, Wall Street knows crypto is the wave of the future. They may say it is all smoke and mirrors, but most of the big banks and firms are setting up their own cryptos and even exchanges to trade them."

"Anna. I think I get Golden Gate, or at least the general idea, which sounds great. I can't imagine anyone not wanting you to succeed. Even corporations and people without a social conscience shouldn't object to the idea, if only so they can burnish their reputations. But that begs the question. Why wipe Kevin's computer and presumably kill him?"

She shrugged.

"Like I said, I don't have a clue. That's your job."

There was another possibility, which I knew she wouldn't like. Nor would Alice. But it had to be said.

"Maybe the files weren't wiped by someone else," I said. "Maybe Kevin knew you would be able to retrieve them and wiped his computer himself. So only you could access them."

Anna looked angry.

"You think Kevin jumped!"

I hesitated. I thought about what Inspector Lin had said about the scream. And I also thought about one word that kept popping up: Billions.

"No, I don't think he killed himself. But we're missing something."

Anna smiled and got up abruptly.

"I want to get more comfortable."

She walked into her bedroom. A moment later, she said, "Alton, can you give me a hand?"

I went into the bedroom. She was standing by the bed, her back to me.

"Can you undo the zipper. I have trouble reaching it."

It occurred to me that she apparently had no trouble zipping it up, but I complied. I pulled the zipper down a few inches.

"A little more, thank you."

I got the zipper about halfway down her back. She wasn't wearing a bra. That wasn't the only undergarment she wasn't wearing. She reached around and finished unzipping. Then, she shrugged out of the dress, which piled at her feet. She kicked it away. And turned around, stark naked.

My initial observation, when she was fully clothed, that she had a taut body perfectly proportional to her diminutive size, had been right on the money. Beneath that cute pixie face, she had a figure that would have launched a thousand aircraft carriers. Small, but high and firm breasts, an almost-washboard midriff, and shaved pudenda. My throat went dry. I tried not to swallow.

Anna put her arms around my neck and her feet on top of my shoes. She still had to go up on her toes, but when she did, she clamped her lips to mine and her tongue slithered into my mouth. She tasted of everything she'd drunk, with an overlay of marijuana. And, of course, of the promise of sex. I heard a familiar roaring in my ears.

Taken by surprise, my arms went instinctively around her. But given the disparity in our height, my hands wound up clasping her muscled buttocks. Her breasts might have been small, but they pressed vigorously against my chest. I could feel her hard nipples. She rubbed herself against one of my legs, buried her head in my neck, shuddered and moaned.

"God," she gasped. "I just came."

I felt myself losing control. At the last possible moment, I squeezed her buttocks, hard.

Anna yelped and her feet came off mine.

"That hurts," she said.

"Believe me, it hurts me more than you," I managed to croak.

"I kind of like it," she purred.

Good Lord.

I put my hands under her arms, lifted her easily, and rather roughly threw her back on the bed.

"Control yourself, Anna. This is not going to happen."

She gave me a sly gaze, looking like Audrey Hepburn in *Breakfast at Tiffany's*. I'd recently watched it on cable. Did anyone ever turn down Audrey Hepburn?

"Are you sure? The weed is great for orgasms."

I felt something. Anna's right foot was massaging my groin. I tried not to look at what was being offered further up her legs and concentrated on the foot.

"Isn't this better than a kick there," she said huskily. "I can tell that you like it. Same foot by the way."

Before her toes could work too much more magic, I grabbed her ankle near its Koala Bear tattoo and twisted it, so that she was forced to roll over on her stomach.

"Oh, I like it this way, too," she said, and began drawing her knees up.

I was pretty sure any way she didn't like "it" hadn't been invented yet. But I'd had enough. I lay on top of her, pressed her flat and pinned her wrists.

"Listen, Anna. I may be the only man on the West Coast who would turn you down, but I am. Thanks for the offer. But I'm spoken for. Now, if I let you up, will you be a good girl?"

She sighed audibly.

"Don't you guys on the East Coast like sex? I love it. With the right man, anyway. Even if you're my uncle. Incest is best, isn't it?"

She giggled and then yawned.

"Oh, well. Be a sweetheart and cover me with the blankets. Then you can go take a cold shower."

I covered her, then leaned down and gave her an uncle-like peck on the top of her head.

She beat a hand against her pillow.

"Damn! Why did they have to kill Kevin?"

I thought she was going to start crying. I'm no good with crying women. But she didn't.

"I'm meeting Sandy for breakfast tomorrow early," she mumbled. "I'll bring you back some croissants."

Going from the promise of endless sex to croissants was quite a segue. She certainly was an interesting girl.

By the time I let myself out of her room, Anna was snoring lightly.

I thought about going for a swim in the bay but settled for the cold shower.

CHAPTER 21 - BOOM

I was still a little wary of the time zone change, so I set my smart-phone alarm for 6:30 AM. That would be 9:30 back in New York. I'd call Alice. I wouldn't mention my near miss with the lovely Anna, but I would bring her up to speed on everything else.

Would she be happier to know that I thought Kevin Allender was probably a murder victim and not a suicide? Dead is dead. I wondered if Alice was so far removed from her ex-husband's life that she wouldn't feel any guilt. I doubted that. She'd feel something. But I thought she could handle a murder better than a suicide. Up to a point, of course. Being tossed out the window of a high-rise couldn't have been pleasant.

I fell asleep. And dreamed. There was a green mist and I was on a large bridge. The Golden Gate? But I was not alone. I was standing next to a woman in a scarf. It was Audrey Hepburn. I was holding something in my hand. It was blue.

"Is that a Tiffany box," Audrey asked.

"No, it's a block," I said.

Audrey, who then morphed into Alice, looked disappointed, so I tossed the block into the void.

***

I needn't have bothered with the alarm. The explosion brought me wide awake.

At first, I assumed it was an earthquake. When you're in San Francisco, that's what is immediately associated with loud noises and a shaking building. But then there was relative silence, punctuated only by the honking of nearby car alarms and the tinkling of glass and other debris on the lanai outside my room. Then I saw a swirl of smoke pass the window and could smell something burning.

I threw on my pants and raced outside, barefoot and bare-chested but oblivious to the morning chill. Other half-dressed people were very cautiously peering out of their condo doorways with frightened looks on their faces. I instinctively glanced toward Anna's condo. The door was still closed.

In her parking spot, what was left of her Lexus was a smoldering wreck. I could see a shriveled, blackened torso behind the steering wheel. My mouth was suddenly dry. I had trouble swallowing. I stumbled over something. I looked down. It was a leg. A woman's leg. A naked, shoe-less women's right leg. It was scorched and missing some toes, but I could clearly see the Koala Bear tattoo on the ankle.

I felt the gorge rise in my throat. A man from one of the condos started toward the Lexus. All my instincts told me to do the same. But I also knew that nothing could be done for what remained of Anna in the Lexus

"Stay back!" I said. "The gas tank may blow."

"Harry, get back here," a woman shouted.

Harry had spunk. He didn't retreat. But he also had brains. He stopped where he was.

"We should call 9-1-1," he said.

I could hear sirens in the distance, warbling closer.

"Somebody already has," I said.

"Whose car was that?"

I was about to reply when someone ran up to me in the morning gloom.

"Alton! Are you OK?"

It was Anna, holding a paper bag. I was momentarily speechless.

"My car! What happened?"

She looked at me.

"Why are you staring at me that way?"

"Anna, where the hell were you?"

"I went down to have breakfast with Sandy."

She held up the bag.

"I brought you back a couple of croissants."

She looked back at what was left of her car. I could see men running up from the administration building. Some appeared to be carrying fire extinguishers.

"Almond," Anna murmured.

"I thought you were dead," I said.

"Oh, sweet Jesus!"

She began to walk toward the SUV, which was still burning furiously. I grabbed her, but not before she spotted the form in the front seat.

"What's that?"

"Don't look, Anna."

She dropped the bag and tried to twist away. I held fast.

"Oh my God! It's Sandy!"

I heard a woman say, "What is that, Harry?"

"Oh, Christ! Oh, Christ!"

"Harry, what?"

"It's a leg!"

"Put it down! Put it down!"

Another woman screamed. I turned.

Harry dropped the leg and vomited.

***

"Sandy told me she was going into Sausalito and didn't have a ride," Anna said, repeating everything I already knew. People in shock often do that. "It was too early for the shuttle, and the guy who lets people borrow a Lexus wasn't in yet. So, I told her to take my car. I was chatting with some of the maintenance guys when we heard the blast."

We were in my room. I'd thrown on a shirt, the collar now damp with her tears, which had mercifully abated.

"When I saw the tattoo on her ankle, I assumed it was you," I said.

"Tattoo?"

"A Koala Bear. Her right ankle."

"You looked in the car? It was burning. How could you see her ankle?"

I didn't know how else to say it, so I just said it.

"Sandy's leg wasn't in the car. It had been blown off."

Anna's eyes widened, but she held it together.

"We flew to Australia together a few months ago. For a week. We had a great time. We thought it was cool to get identical tats. Guy in Melbourne did them. But hers was on her left ankle. Didn't you notice?"

I didn't know what to say to that. I had basically just been blown out of bed and was half-asleep when I saw the leg. *All legs look alike to me* wouldn't cut it, so I kept my mouth shut. It's something I should do more often.

Anna gave me a wan smile.

"Men," she said, shaking her head.

"I'm just happy you are OK, Anna."

"At first we thought it was the start of an earthquake," she said.

For some reason I was relieved that I hadn't been the only one to jump to that conclusion.

"It was a bomb, wasn't it?"

If it wasn't a bomb, I thought to myself, there is going to be a massive Lexus recall. I also now knew that Allender had definitely not killed himself. Someone wanted him dead, and also wanted Anna dead. And it was someone who had professional help.

"Yes. It was a bomb. Probably wired to the ignition."

She swallowed.

"And it was meant for me."

There was a loud rap on the door.

"That's probably the cops," I said. "I'm surprised it took them so long."

Anna gripped my arm.

"What should I tell them?"

"The truth will set you free. But I might leave out the part where you burgled Allender's apartment."

"But his murder and the car bomb have to be connected!"

"Can you prove that?"

She thought that over.

"No. But it's obvious."

"Obvious to us, maybe. But cops don't like obvious. They like proof, and evidence."

"Are you crazy? Like the car bomb isn't evidence?"

"Sure. But they don't have evidence that Allender was murdered. Yet. They have a body. Sandy's.

They'll know it was a bomb straight away. They'll know it was probably you that it was meant for, but they will also run down all the leads relating to Sandy. Maybe she told someone she was taking your car. Even you will be a suspect. And me."

"Us! That's crazy, too."

"We know that, and they will eliminate us quickly. When you tell them about Allender's death, they'll have their hands full. Allender was cremated, so they'll hit a dead end there. I suspect they won't get anywhere with the bomb, either. If it was terrorism, perhaps. They'd bring in the F.B.I. and Homeland to trace the bomb parts. Maybe they'll do that at some point if they are stumped. But that will take time. Meanwhile, you are in danger until they connect the dots. And I don't think the people involved in this will wait for that."

It took a moment for that to sink in. Anna let go of my arms as her hand went to her mouth.

"Oh, Jesus!"

"Don't worry, kid. I'm not going to let anything happen to you. I'm going to beat the cops to whoever is behind this."

"But where will you start?"

"I've got a pretty good idea, but the less you know the better."

She looked as if she wanted to say something else, but just then the door knocking became more insistent.

"Sausalito police! Open up!"

"Not smart to piss off the cops," I said. "But they're local. Don't tell them everything you know or suspect. I want to talk to Lin."

Anna gave me a blank look.

"The San Francisco cop I told you about. He caught Allender's alleged suicide. Lin is a sharp cookie."

"What about these cops? Can't we get into trouble for withholding evidence?"

"Again, what evidence? Besides, we've got bigger things to worry about."

The truth was, I withhold evidence from the authorities all the time. Most private eyes do. It goes with the job.

I went to let the police in.

CHAPTER 22 - GETTING OUT OF DODGE

The Sausalito cops kept at us most of the morning, finally cutting us loose just after noon. It did not appear they believed much of what we told them.

After they left, Anna and I sat and talked in my room.

"I think you have to get out of San Francisco," I said. "At least until I figure out what the hell is going on."

She didn't say anything, just stared out the window.

"Anna?"

She looked at me.

"Where can I go? I don't have any family."

"None?"

"I'm an orphan. My adoptive parents are both dead. Wonderful people. Farm couple in Missouri. Skimped and saved to send me to college and then grad school. They were driving out here to see me when a semi crossed a divider in the interstate and killed them. They didn't have any other children. I may have some cousins somewhere, but I don't keep in touch."

"I'm sorry, Anna. But it would probably be a bad idea to stay with relatives anyway. It's the first place someone would look for you."

"Then, what now?"

"I can find you someplace safe."

I told Anna to get a few of her things together, anything she could fit in a backpack. While she packed, I called Arman Rahm.

"I need a place to stash a young woman."

"Don't we all. And, of course, you thought of me."

"When you need the very best…"

He laughed.

"I presume safety is paramount."

"Someone tried to blow her up. I think the same people who probably aced Alice's ex. She worked with him."

There was a pause.

"So, Alice was right in her suspicions."

I heard a harsh grunt in the background. Kalugin.

"Anything else you can tell me?"

"Nothing concrete. I'm flying blind out here."

"What happens if someone blows you up?"

"I haven't thought that far ahead."

"Do you ever?"

"Skip the lecture. Can you help me out here, or not?"

"Of course. I know just the place. Put the mystery woman on a plane to Miami, via Orlando, with a layover. Text me the details. But tell her to deplane in Orlando. I'll have someone meet her there."

"Arman, I don't know how good these guys out here are."

"That's why it's better that you don't know her final destination. Don't worry about her. Where she's going there are people who will keep an eye on her. They are very security conscious. Hold on."

I heard a garbled conversation on Arman's end.

"Maks wants to know if Alice is in danger."

"I don't think so."

"Just the same, he wants to keep an eye on her."

I didn't argue. Kalugin would make sure nothing happened to Alice.

***

Anna and I went down to speak to the bigwigs at the Cavallo Point resort. They were shaken up, of course, and in shock over the death of a popular employee. But they were also anxious to put a PR disaster behind them. Resort explosions, not to mention murder, are bad for business. Not something for the brochure. So, they bought my plan.

An hour later, three identical Lexuses left Cavallo Point simultaneously, all headed to San Francisco, all with two passengers, a man and a woman. I drove Anna in the middle car; resort management volunteers, vouched for by a nervous Anna, in the other vehicles. Our little caravan split up in downtown San Francisco, weaving through city streets to discourage any tail. Anna was carrying only a backpack.

We ended up at San Francisco International. I was sure we were not followed. My driving was so random I couldn't have tailed myself. I knew somebody could track the car's GPS system. So, I didn't use it and let Anna direct me. And I parked in a lot at a terminal different from the one we wanted. One that serviced international flights.

"Give me your cell phone."

I dropped it in a trash bin as we walked to a tram. If someone tracked her phone, they might assume Anna caught a flight overseas. By the time they found out she didn't, she'd be long gone elsewhere.

"Buy burner phones when you land. Or use the ones the people who meet your plane may give you.

I'm sure they will be untraceable."

I had told Anna of my arrangement with Arman Rahm.

"Who are these people?"

"Friends."

We took a tram to the correct terminal.

Anna felt bad about missing Sandy's funeral.

"She was my best friend," Anna said, tearfully. "And I'm the reason she's dead."

"You are fortunate it's not your own funeral, kid. And cut the bullshit about guilt. The only one responsible for Sandy's murder is the guy that planted the bomb. Now, remember, don't contact anyone. No one. No friends, not even me. If something happens to me before I get this all straightened out, the people you are with will know what to do."

"Will they go to the police?"

"Sure," I said, wondering if Arman would.

"I don't like running away. I don't want anything to happen to you on my account."

"I'm not doing this only for you, Anna. I like working alone. This way I won't have to worry about you."

Anna saw the logic of my plan. We bought her ticket to Miami and I went over what she was to do in Orlando. Just before she checked through security, she turned and kissed me.

"Take care of yourself," she said and quickly walked away.

***

I went to the other terminal parking lot and retrieved the Lexus. I have to admit I instinctively hesitated when pushing the ignition button. I drove back to Cavallo Point, packed and went to check out. The receptionist said that my stay was "comped". I got the impression that management was glad to see me go, and, hopefully, never return. I ordered up an Uber and headed into San Francisco, calling Inspector Lin while on the Golden Gate. I was pretty sure he'd give us a slide on not telling the local fuzz everything we suspected. He was a big city cop. He'd jump at the chance to link Allender's death to the car bomb when I told him about it. I knew he could finesse Anna's burglary.

I'd just started to tell him what happened when he abruptly cut me off.

"I'm tied up right now," he said. "I'll text you my home address. I get off at 4. I'll meet you there at 5."

He hung up. My iPhone beeped. The address. Lin's house was in Sausalito, which I'd just left. Wonderful. When we exited the Golden Gate on the San Francisco side I told the driver to meander around a while in a maze of hilly side streets.

"I'm a tourist," I deadpanned. "Take your time and I'll make it worth your while."

If anyone had been following me, they'd assume I was being canny. Or nuts. I looked at my watch. I had plenty of time before meeting Lin and was hungry. San Francisco is like Paris. You have to try really hard to find a bad meal, especially if you avoid the touristy areas. I'd already convinced the driver I was a rube, so I queried my GPS for any great Italian restaurants not on Fisherman's Wharf and gave my driver an address.

"Da Flora," he said, after noting the destination, "is

one of the best little Italian restaurants in the city."

"Lucky guess," I said.

It was a nice little place, with a blackboard menu and everything homemade. I was soon drinking a decent Chianti and eating some of the best spaghetti Bolognese I'd ever had. I lingered over coffee and cannoli.

Fully sated, I took a Lyft back to Sausalito.

Someone was hunting Annalise Purna.

But now I was also going to do some hunting.

CHAPTER 23 - LESLIE

Inspector Lin lived on Harrison Avenue. From what I knew about Saucilito housing, the neighborhood didn't look like any cop, of any rank, including Commissioner, could afford to live there. Custom homes were the norm, with architectural styles ranging from wooded hillside Victorian estates to modern waterfront villas. Lin's was a two-level contemporary that sloped down toward the town and bay beyond it.

There were two cars parked next to each other in the driveway outside a large garage. One was a silver Ford Explorer. The other was a red Lamborghini convertible. I may have imagined it, but the Explorer looked embarrassed. I wouldn't have blamed it.

I walked up a short path from the driveway, passing two small kid's bicycles, one blue and the other, pink. I rang the doorbell and a tall and very handsome black man opened it. With his shaved head and middleweight's toned physique he looked vaguely familiar, but I couldn't place him.

"Mr. Rhode?"

"Yes."

He put out his hand and we shook.

"I'm Vivian Hayden. Charles told me you were stopping by. He's in the shower. He just got back from a run. He'll be down in a minute."

"Vivian" was the "babe" Lin had spoken to on the phone that day in the squad room. I thought I did pretty good hiding my surprise.

Hayden led me through living and entertaining

spaces, full of expensive-looking white- leather and chrome furniture. The rooms seamlessly transitioned to a magnificent outdoor teak deck overlooking San Francisco Bay. The view could only be described as spectacular. The deck and everything on it were spotless and appeared to be built to exacting standards.

I couldn't help but think of my deck at home, built by moonlighting firemen to sturdy but inexpensive standards and bolted to my house quite illegally according to the New York City Building Department, which wouldn't know about it until I sold. I'd cross that bridge, or deck, when it happened.

"That's some view," I said.

Hayden took a moment to point out Belvedere Island, Angel Island, Berkeley, Oakland, the Oakland Bay Bridge, Alcatraz and Treasure Island.

"But enough tourism braggadocio," he said. "How about a drink? I'm going to have a gin-and-tonic, with a lime, but we have everything."

"A gin-and-tonic is fine."

There was a wet bar just outside the deck sliders, with a full sideboard setup, and Hayden made the drinks efficiently, gave me mine and sat in a wicker chair across from me, crossing one leg over the other. He was wearing a white shirt, pale-blue sweater and tan pants. He was shod in brown tasseled loafers with no socks. A tray of nuts and cheeses was on a small glass-top table between our Adirondack chairs.

Hayden made no move to eat, so neither did I. It was sunny but cool, with a good breeze off the bay. I envied him his sweater. I wouldn't have thought of entertaining a visitor outside, but maybe that's what they did in this part of Northern California. Especially when they could show off the view. It was certainly nothing I couldn't handle, especially with a drink in hand.

"You were expecting a woman, weren't you?"

So much for hiding my surprise. I felt like a prize idiot, having been fooled by another unisex name. I'd have to tell Abby when I got home. I tried to regroup.

"You got me. I heard Lin talking to you on the phone. He sounded so, I don't know, domestic. And then he gave me marriage advice. I leapt to the wrong conclusion. Sorry."

"We're not."

"I'm sure. And your name does go both ways."

"Well, I don't."

"I didn't mean…"

He laughed.

"I'm busting your balls, Mr. Rhode."

"You're doing a hell of a job." We raised glasses to each other and drank. "But you make a hell of a drink."

"I use Bombay Sapphire," Hayden said. "It's 94 proof. Some people find it a bit stronger than regular gin. I cut it with a dash of Angostura."

He was right about the gin. A couple of these and I wouldn't feel an Arctic blast.

"Bitters make it better," I said.

Hayden chuckled.

"I like that. Who said it?"

"As far as I know, no one. I just made it up."

"That's wonderful. Do you mind if I steal it? It's perfect for my character."

Then it hit me. I knew who he was. *That* Vivian Hayden.

"You are an actor," I said. "The TV remake of *Streets of San Francisco*. You play what's his name. The cop Michael Douglas played in the original."

"Yeah, I'm a black Steve Keller. They wanted to make him gay, too. But I told them black was enough of a switch. Then they suggested transgender. Jesus! Why not put him in a wheelchair and cover all the bases. I won. I'm an actor. I can play straight."

"You fooled me," I teased.

"Touché," Hayden said and laughed. "We just got picked up for another season. You watch it?"

"Sometimes. Good show."

What else could I say? That I came across some episodes while channel surfing during Yankee rain delays and watched for only 10 minutes? Or that I preferred the original, even though I barely remembered it? But at least the Lamborghini was explained.

"Movies, too, right? One of the *Mission Impossibles*?"

Hayden was pleased.

"That's right. The fourth one. Played a C.I.A. agent who helps Ethan Hunt. That's the role that got me Keller."

Hayden waved his free hand around.

"The role that got us this house."

"Maybe you will be the next Michael Douglas."

"From your lips to God's ears," Hayden said, with a laugh. Dramatic pause. "I hear he gets all the girls."

I liked Hayden.

"I have to ask you," I said. "Does Tom Cruise really do his own stunts?"

Hayden smiled.

"If I tell you, I'll have to kill you."

We both laughed.

"Truth is, yeah, most of them. He scared the hell out of me. Even with safety wires, which are edited out, and C.G.I. stuff, Tom pushes the envelope. He gets hurt a lot. But he's a trooper. And a much better actor than most people realize."

"I always thought so."

Just then, two children, a boy and a girl, ran noisily out onto the desk, followed by a big yellow Labrador Retriever, who came right up to me and sniffed me suspiciously. I was obviously not a threat, but good dogs don't take chances, especially when they are herding *their* kids. I put out my hand, fingers closed, and the Lab sniffed my fist.

"That's Monarch," Hayden said. "He won't hurt you. Give him a piece of cheese and he's yours forever."

I did.

"Charles says we shouldn't feed him people food," the young girl said. "He'll get spoiled."

"Especially cheese," the boy said. "He gets consecrated."

The girl looked at me and rolled her eyes.

"He means constipated."

She was maybe seven, and dark-skinned, but not in the way African-Americans are. I guessed South American. She had small, sharp features and slick black hair. The word Aztec came to mind. It's too early to really tell with a child that young, but she would probably be a real beauty when she grew up.

"He's spoiled already, Jazz," Hayden replied. "By the way, this is Jasmine. And her brother is Jared. Say hello to Mr. Rhode, kids. He's a private detective."

Both children shook hands with me. You don't see that very often.

"Our dad is a police inspector, and our other dad plays one on TV," Jasmine said. "Did you know that?"

"Yes, I did."

"Are you a real detective?" Jared asked. "Or a make-believe detective, like Vivian?"

"Sometimes I'm not sure," I said.

Jared was white, maybe a year older than his sister. Fair-skinned and blond-haired, and handsome now, and would stay that way. He looked German, or perhaps Swedish.

Both kids started peppering me with questions, until Hayden intervened.

"OK, kids. Give Mr. Rhode a break. He's here on business. Why don't you take Monarch into the playroom? I'm sure you can find a video game."

He lowered his voice ominously.

"Or would you rather start your homework?"

Both kids shot off the deck. Monarch, to his credit choosing the kids over cheese, was in hot pursuit, the nails on his paws scraping on the teak. Hayden and I both laughed.

"Works like a charm," he said.

"What works like a charm?"

It was Charles Lin, just walking out to the deck. Without asking, Hayden started mixing drinks for all of us, and explained the remark.

"Really, Vivian, you're going to spoil the both of them."

"I let Monarch eat a piece of cheese, too," Hayden said. "Arrest me."

"I'm off duty," Lin said, smiling, and sat in another chair.

CHAPTER 24 - PRESSURE

When we all had our drinks, we started picking at the cheese platter. Why should Monarch have all the fun?

"The kids are great," I said. "Smart as whips."

"Thank you," Lin said. "They do have their moments, especially when there are no guests around. Jazz can be bossy, and she and Jared sometimes fight like cats and dogs. Poor Monarch is very conflicted. But they are good kids and we were very lucky to be able to adopt two children so near in age."

"Thank God we live in San Francisco," Hayden added. "Both Jazz and Jared came from broken homes, parents on drugs. We got them young, before any real damage was done to them."

"They seem to be thriving," I said. "Despite the cheese."

Both fathers laughed.

"Are you two married?"

They looked at each other and smiled.

"Next month," Lee said. "We wanted to wait until Vivian got settled in his show."

"Congratulations."

"Well," Hayden said, "I think I'll go check on the kids. You two have business to discuss. Nice meeting you Alton. Don't get up."

I did anyway and shook his hand. He left, shutting the French doors behind him. I sat back down.

"Nice guy," I said. "Been together long?"

"Almost 10 years. Viv was a struggling actor working as a waiter when we met. Somebody got stabbed in his restaurant and he was a witness."

"Every cloud has a silver lining," I said.

Lin smiled.

"We haven't always lived this grandly."

He paused.

"I bet when you first got here you thought I had to be on the take."

"I wondered about that, especially when I saw the Lamborghini. Then I recognized who Vivian was."

"His latest toy. Mostly he takes it to work. Rest of the time we're in the SUV, playing soccer dads."

Lin took a long pull of his drink.

"I wasn't tied up at work."

Lin looked uncomfortable.

"I've been taken off the case. I didn't want to talk about Allender over the phone."

So that was why we were freezing our asses off on the deck.

"I didn't know it was a case."

"Well, whatever you want to call it, or whatever you were going to tell me, I'm no longer on it. Nobody is. Kevin Allender committed suicide, and that's that."

Lin got up to freshen his drink. He nodded at my glass. I shook my head. A big container ship in the bay headed toward the docks in Oakland. I wondered what goods were in the containers and whether they would now cost Americans more. Two seagulls cruised by the house, tariff-free.

"Somebody wants it to be a suicide," I said.

"Maybe it was. Lots of people jump out of buildings in San Francisco, especially since they put up those anti-suicide nets under the Golden Gate. Not long ago some babe took a header from the 42nd floor of the Lumina. A murder-suicide."*

*(*The murder-suicide Lin refers to occurred in CHANCE, a Jake Scarne thriller by the same author.)*

* * *

"I saw that on the news," I said. "She was some New York billionaire's girlfriend, right."

"Yeah. They were going to be married and she stabbed him to death for no apparent reason and then did a Peter Pan off the ledge. Landed on a cab. Looked like she was asleep. Photo went viral."

I remembered the photos of the dead girl. She had been beautiful. With everything to live for. There had been talk of drugs, as there always is when something horrible happens to the rich and famous. Then, as now, I thought it was a terrible tragedy.

"Point is," Lin continued, "you never know what goes through someone's mind."

I wasn't going to be deterred.

"I don't think Allender killed himself."

Lin held up his hand.

"I don't want to hear about it."

Lin sat back down. He looked miserable. And worried. There was little or no chance of being bugged out on the deck. And yet Lin still didn't want to stay involved. It made me wonder what I had gotten myself into.

"Rhode, I'm a good cop. It's all I've ever wanted to be. I work in the best station in Frisco. Vivian and I have two great kids and live in a great neighborhood. I can't risk all of it. I can't risk any of it. Not in this political environment. We are lucky to be gay in the most liberal city in America. But that can change in a second in today's political environment. Vivian is doing well, but Hollywood careers can evaporate quickly. I don't want to be reduced to writing parking tickets in Polk Gulch."

I didn't know where Polk Gulch was, but I assumed it wasn't anything like Nob Hill.

"That's what they threatened you with?"

Lin shook his head.

"They didn't have to. When they told me to wrap it up, I asked command why. I was told to just follow orders. I pushed a bit, with some friends higher up, and it was made clear that someone very powerful doesn't want anyone looking into Allender. Officially."

I caught the word, "officially".

"So, where does that leave us?"

"There is no 'us'. Only you."

"Who doesn't have to follow orders."

Lin shrugged.

"Well, thanks for the drinks, Inspector."

Lin stood.

"You're welcome to stay for dinner. It's mac-and-cheese night. Vivian makes it from scratch."

Bolognese and macaroni-and-cheese in the same day didn't cut it, so I politely declined. Lin seemed relieved.

"I'll see you out."

As we walked through the house, I took out my smart phone and hit my Uber app. I wasn't being paranoid. I'm still undecided about which taxi service is the best, so I alternate.

A slew of little car blips, looking like hungry black insects, filled the screen, all within a few blocks of the red dot that signified my location. Sausalito was apparently a hot spot for Uber drivers. I chose a car that was three minutes away.

Lin and I passed a door that presumably led to a lower floor. I could hear what sounded like machine gun fire. Then an explosion. And children laughing.

I heard Vivian Hayden say, "that's not fair."

"Jasmine and Jared are whipping his butt in a video game," Lin said.

CHAPTER 25 - CRABBY

"You going to drop this?"

We were standing at the curb. A black SUV turned the corner towards us. My Uber.

"Can't," I said.

"Can I can give you a bit of advice, Rhode?"

"Which is?"

"Watch your back. There are a lot of high rises and windows in San Francisco."

"I'll keep that in mind."

Lin shook his head in apparent resignation.

"Tell your driver to take you to Salito's. Has the best Dungeness crab in the city. It will be crowded, but mention Vivian's name and they'll take care of you. He's a regular there."

"Not you?"

"Of course, but my name won't get you a table. He's a celebrity."

"Except when Jared and Jasmine play a video game with him," I said.

"You have that right," Lin said, smiling.

We shook hands and I got into the SUV.

Lin tapped on the window. I rolled it down.

"Remember what I told you," Lin said.

He paused.

"But if you don't get yourself killed, I might want to hear what you've found out."

Great. Alive and with proof, I might prove useful to the S.F.P.D.

I looked back at Lin as we drove away. He was staring at my Uber. I turned to my driver, a middle-aged woman with pictures of what I guessed were her grandkids under the flap of her visor. I asked her to take me to the restaurant instead of my hotel, which was the original address I put in when I sent for the Uber.

"You know it?"

"Sure. It's here in Sausalito. Get it. Salito's. About five minutes away."

Which meant that my fare would be a lot cheaper. I don't like stiffing grandmothers.

"I'll pay the fare I signed up for."

"You don't have to do that, sir. I'll probably get a fare from the restaurant."

"OK. But even if you do, you won't fight me on a big tip, right?"

"Don't like to fight with customers, sir," she said, laughing, as she searched her computer screen for her next fare.

I resisted the urge to say, "Follow that blip!"

Salito's was on the water, as part of a bustling marina. Water, hawsers and seagulls lapped, strained and perched respectively. I was hungry and my stomach rumbled in concert as the aroma of cooked crab wafted into my Uber. I suspected that Inspector Lin was proving useful in the dinner department, if nothing else.

A couple was waiting outside to change places with me. The man was bald, short and dumpy, with a red face that would have given a lobster a run for its money. The woman was tall, blond, willowy and half his age. His pot belly brushed me as he bulled past me into the cab. He didn't even wait for the woman. I got a whiff of his breath: Seafood, with a strong overlay of booze.

"You took your fuckin' time gettin' out of the cab, pal."

"I wanted to tip the driver," I said.

"It's a fuckin' Uber, pal. You don't have to tip these people. What are you, a tourist?"

He tumbled into the car. I looked at the woman. She was a stunner. She was shaking her head and smiling ruefully. I winked and politely held the door for her. As she got in the car, she slipped something into my palm and whispered, "He's a client."

I heard short-and-dumpy say "fuckin' tourist" and then growl at the driver. I was glad I'd tipped her heavily.

The Uber drove away and I looked in my palm. It was a business card. In bold script it said "Discreet Escort Service". There was a phone number and a name, "Evelyn". I was happy she wasn't lobster-head's wife or significant other. Maybe he'd pass out before the nasty business.

I went into the restaurant. It was crowded and loud, obviously a local hot spot. There was both indoor-and-outdoor seating, and people waiting for a table. I didn't have to use Hayden's name because I found a seat at the bar, where I like to eat when I can if dining alone. Most everyone there was waiting for a table, but when I asked for a menu the bartender set down a place mat and utensils and people politely gave me some extra room. It was a happy crowd, a sign of a good restaurant. I hoped that short-and-dumpy at least had behaved himself at dinner. Although I doubted it.

I ordered a pint of Laguinitas and took out the escort service business card. I crumpled it and dropped it among the detritus on a passing busboy's tray.

The Dungeness, swathed in hot butter and washed down with another pint of cold beer, was everything a seafood meal should be. Almost as good as the stone crabs I'd had in southern Florida in the past.

As always when I eat a great meal by myself, I thought of how wonderful it would have been to share it with Alice. I'm always conflicted at good restaurants, and have trouble making up my mind among a slew of potential selections. She would have ordered something I also liked, so I could have a taste. Which would wind up being half her plate.

More important, Alice would be animated and beautiful. Our conversation would be stimulating. In a seafood restaurant she'd undoubtedly make jokes about oysters and my libido. She would drop hints of postprandial carnal delights to come. People walking by us would glance at her. The men would think that I was a lucky devil.

If Alice were with me, I'd have dropped Vivian's name like an anvil to get the best table in the joint.

After dinner, I took another Uber back to the Westin St. Francis. The same woman who had initially checked me in remembered me fondly. Or at least, politely.

"How long will you be with us this time, Mr. Rhode?"

"It may be a while. Can you arrange a rental car for me?"

I suspected that having a car handy would be wise.

Getting shot while waiting for an Uber or Lyft is unprofessional in my business.

"Of course. We have several agencies on site. Do you have a preference?"

"No. A standard sedan would be fine. With a GPS system. And I'd prefer a car that does not blow up."

Her smile never wavered.

"Not a problem, sir. How soon will you be needing it?"

"Tomorrow morning will be fine."

"Just stop by the desk and we will have you all fixed up."

I thanked her, collected my key and headed to the elevators. I needed a good night's sleep. It was going to be a busy day tomorrow.

CHAPTER 26 - MUPPETS REDUX

I slept like a baby. When I got up, I found my way to the hotel gym and worked every machine but the leg press. I hate the leg press. I keep hitting myself in the chin with my knees. By the time I got back to my room, I was sweating rivulets despite the air-conditioning, which was set somewhere near absolute zero. I showered, shaved and dressed and headed to the lobby at 9 AM.

It was time to shake things up. In a case with few clues and no real suspects, sometimes throwing a hand grenade can be productive. From chaos often comes a lead. So, I grabbed a coffee and an egg sandwich from the cafe on the ground floor and picked up my rental, a dark-blue Nissan Altima, in the hotel garage.

I decided to revisit Allender's old office. I wanted to talk to Barry Smith again.

He wasn't there. In fact, nobody was there, even a temp receptionist. A sign taped to the door said the space was for lease and anyone interested should contact the real estate division of Kursk Integrity Bank. There were several phone numbers. I called one and asked for Barry Smith.

A nice young woman on the other end told me that Smith did not work in the real estate division.

"I know," I said. "But I'm wondering how I can reach him. This is the only number I have at the moment."

"You should try the main office on Mission Street. Mr. Smith is the managing director of the bank. I can give you their number, if you like."

I took it, mostly to make her happy. I could find the bank. I wanted to see Smith in person. I wanted to ask him why the managing director of Kursk took such an interest in closing up Kevin Allender's office, a man he worked closely with but said he hardly knew.

Using the Nissan's GPS, I found the Kursk headquarters easily enough on Mission Street. The building was old but the lobby was modernly decked out. It was very bright and cheerful, with a lot of people at desks looking busy. But I didn't see any traditional banking going on. No tellers, no lines, no guards.

I approached a large desk with two signs. One said, "Receptionist". The other, bigger, sign said, "VISITORS MUST CHECK IN!"

A young woman at the desk smiled cheerfully at me.

"May I help you?"

"Is this a bank?"

"Of course."

She didn't add "silly," but it was there on her innocent face as her smile widened.

"It doesn't look like a bank. If I wanted to rob it, how would I do it?"

She furrowed her brow.

"This is the bank's headquarters. I guess you would have to visit one of our branch offices, sir. Or open up an account on line."

Cheerful for sure, but she wasn't as bright as the lobby. She handed me a brochure.

"You can find everything you want in this," she said.

"Can I find Barry Smith in here," I said, leafing through the brochure.

"Pardon me."

"I came to see Barry Smith. I was told he might be here."

"The executive offices are on the fourth floor. But you would need a visitor's pass to go up there."

"And where do I get one."

"From me."

"May I have one?"

"Do you have an appointment?"

"No."

"You need an appointment to get a visitor's pass."

She seemed like a nice kid, but very wet behind the ears. I took out my wallet and quickly flashed my N.Y.P.D. credentials before snapping it shut.

"This is police business, Miss," I said brusquely. "I don't need a pass."

I almost said "no stinkin' pass" but that would have been overdoing it. But I gave the poor kid my best cop stare.

"And don't let anyone know I'm coming. Do you understand?"

"Yes, officer. The elevators are over there. Mr. Smith's office will be down the hall to your right."

I thanked her, smiling in a way that I hoped convinced her that if she followed my orders she was not going to Alcatraz, or its modern equivalent.

When I got to the fourth floor, I walked down a hallway past numerous offices with vice presidents of something or other behind their closed doors. Finally, I came to a suite of offices at the end. The stenciling on the double doors said: *Barry Smith, Managing Director*. I went in.

There was a very large and extremely ugly older woman sitting at a desk outside an inner office. I know that calling a woman ugly is not politically correct. But she would have been ugly as a man, or, for that matter, a British bulldog. She had a face that would sink a thousand ships. Tortoise-shell horn-rimmed glasses hung from a chain around a neck that looked like it belonged to a San Francisco Forty-Niner lineman.

At first, I thought she was wearing a steel-gray helmet, until I realized it was her hair, plastered to her scalp. I knew I was in trouble. She was no cupcake like the girl in the lobby.

"I would like to see Mr. Smith."

"And you are?"

Her voice reminded me of those anti-smoking commercials on TV, where people place artificial voice-box gizmos on their neck.

"Miles Archer, Hudson Bay Insurance."

She pursed her lips at the word "insurance". Now, she looked like a constipated walrus.

"Do you have an appointment?"

"No."

She knew how to deal with an insurance man who lacked an appointment.

"Mr. Smith is a very busy man. Just leave your card."

"He already has my card. I spoke to him recently."

She gave me a look that said, "It wasn't on my watch."

"Just leave your card."

I sighed.

"I bet you have a drawer full of business cards that Smith will never see. For all I care, you can wipe your ass with them. Tell your boss that Miles Archer, the investigator from Hudson Bay, has a few questions about some missing beaver pelts."

She looked like she was going to explode.

"And make it snappy, sister."

She huffed into Smith's office. Then, she came out.

"Mr. Smith will see you," she said, icily.

I walked past her, fully expecting her to bite me. I wondered if my shots were up to date.

Smith was sitting behind a wooden desk the size of Delaware. Two men sat on a couch off to his right, in front of a wall-to wall bookcase. On the opposite wall were a group of video monitors and televisions. The two men looked at me curiously, as if trying to place me. It didn't look as if they were having success.

I wasn't surprised. They had been paying more attention to Anna at the Farley. I was just a guy she was talking to at the bar. But I knew them. Bert and Ernie. Still in ill-fitting green suits.

"Archer, what's this nonsense about beaver pelts? And what did you say to Tiffany? She seemed quite upset."

Tiffany?

I looked at Bert and Ernie.

"I'd rather talk in private."

Smith jerked his head at the two men, who got up and walked past me, staring at me intently but still with no sign of recognition. I heard the door close behind me. There were two plush leather chairs arrayed in front of the desk. Without being asked, I sat in one.

"Where did you get those guys," I said, "Henchmen-R-Us?"

"What do you want, Mr. Archer?"

"My name is not Miles Archer, who, in case you are ever on *Jeopardy*, was Sam Spade's partner in *The Maltese Falcon*."

"Then who the hell are you?"

"My name is Alton Rhode. I'm a private investigator."

I threw one of my business cards on his desk.

"Don't lose that. I don't have many real ones."

"So, you gained entrance under false pretenses."

"That's redundant, Barry. But true. I think I would probably make a great banker. Now, why did you lie about hardly knowing Kevin Allender? I'm looking into his murder."

"Murder? Allender killed himself."

"Nope. Now answer the question."

Smith sat back and put his feet on the desk to show that he didn't take me seriously.

"It was none of your business. I thought you worked for an insurance company."

"Which made the falsehood even worse. There was no reason to lie. Unless you're hiding something."

Smith knew I had him. He was silent. I had already pulled the pin, so now I threw the grenade.

"And why were those two mooks tailing Annalise Purna? Or don't you know her, either?"

"What do you mean, tailing?"

"They were in the Farley bar at Cavallo Point the night before someone tried to kill her."

"I have no idea what you are talking about. I don't keep track of my associates drinking habits. The Farley is a popular place. I'm sure it was a coincidence."

Feigning ignorance is the first defense of a liar. Next, Smith would go the lawyer route.

"Your associates? Those two might rob a bank, but they sure as hell don't work for one. They must have graduated summa cum thug. What's going on, Barry? Why all the obfuscations?"

I just like the word.

"The what?"

"Smokescreens, muddying the water, bullshit."

"This interview is over," Smith said.

His feet came off the desk and he stood.

"From now on, you can talk to our lawyers."

"Right on time," I said.

"Excuse me."

"See you around, Barry."

When I walked out, I passed Bert and Ernie, who were standing next to Miss Walrus. The gruesome threesome. I wanted to whip out my smart phone and take a picture of them together for the grandkids but thought better of it.

"See you all around. I'll be sure to buy your first album. Nice meeting you, Tiffany. Try more roughage."

"Go fuck yourself," she said.

"Do I know you?" Ernie asked.

"The Farley," I said in passing.

I had my back to them but heard him say, "dermo"! Almost simultaneously Bert said "shit"!

It meant the same in Russian and English.

CHAPTER 27 - FACETIME

I next called Arman Rahm.

"Has anyone tried to blow you up lately?"

"I wasn't the target."

"Give them time."

"I appreciate what you did for Anna, Arman. I have another favor to ask."

"Not a problem. I'm between schemes."

"I seem to be running into a lot of Russians out here," I said.

"Aha."

"Aha?"

"The reason for your call is becoming clearer."

"Maybe I just want your recipe for pierogi."

"Pierogi is a Polish treat."

"You guys invaded them so many times and didn't get the recipe?"

Arman laughed.

"Did you know that Russia and San Francisco have an interesting history," he said. "During the San Francisco earthquake in 1906 there was a Russian warship making a port call in the harbor. Its crew provided aid to the citizens."

"I did know that. In fact, your father reminded me of that fact not too long ago."

"He would. He is a proud Russian. Loves history."

"These Russians are bankers and thugs."

"What's the difference?"

"Good point."

I told him about my latest meeting with Barry Smith, and his lies. And Bert and Ernie.

"If you are right, my friend, they've put a target on your back."

"I'm hoping someone makes a stupid move."

"You mean, someone other than you?"

"Always a critic. Can you find out about Kursk? It's Russian owned and seems to be making a lot of inroads and is stepping on a lot of toes, particularly Wells Fargo's, although that probably doesn't break too many hearts out here."

"I should think not. Kursk! Cheeky bastards. They named it after a famous battle in World War II, outside the city of Kursk, where the Red Army tore the guts out of the Nazis. Everyone thinks Stalingrad was the turning point. But after the Battle of Kursk, the Germans were finished. Next stop, Berlin."

"Maybe they just named it after the city."

"No. The German name for the battle was "Citadel".

"Will there be a quiz later, Arman?"

He laughed again.

"I'll call you back, Alton. Do you have Facetime on your smart phone?"

"Yes."

"Good. I like Facetime."

Facetime?

***

Arman called me back two hours later. His face filled my smart phone screen.

"My father would like to speak to you."

He walked over to a table in what I recalled was the kitchen in the Rahm mansion in the Todt Hill section of Staten Island. His father, Marat came into focus, sitting at the island in the kitchen, wearing what looked like the runner-up in an ugly sweater contest. Even though we were separated by a continent, I wisely didn't make a sartorial comment. Arman sat beside him. Maks Kalugin leaned against a nearby counter behind them. It took me a second to realize that no one was apparently holding a smart phone at their end.

"Do you like our new toy," Arman said. "It is a smart phone gimbal stabilizer that allows one to move around the room and stay in focus."

"I didn't realize you were so technologically savvy."

"Russians love the new technologies."

"I guess I know that. You stole our last election."

"Those were Russian Russians. We're American Russians. And in case you are interested, my vote in the last election didn't count, either."

"Move to Idaho."

"A red state. Funny, a generation ago, red was synonymous with Communists. Now, with Conservatism. Anyway, too few people. And too far from the ocean. Russians can't stand to be landlocked."

"How are you, Alton? You are looking well."

It was Marat. Older and thinner, but still vital. As he spoke, the picture focus, presumably sensitive to voice, shifted slightly toward him.

"I'm fine. And you?"

"I just buried my latest doctor. Natural causes, I should add."

I laughed.

"How was your trip to Italy, Mr. Rahm?"

"Wonderful. My grandson is a charming little devil. Now, Arman tells me you are having trouble with some Russians in San Francisco."

"Not exactly trouble. But they may be involved in a murder that the local authorities don't seem to be too interested in pursuing."

"Arman told me it's personal with you. Because of your Alice."

"Yes."

"So, you will pursue it."

"Yes."

Marat Rahm nodded to Kalugin, who filled the coffee cup in front of him.

"Alton says Russian bankers are consolidating their power in San Francisco," Arman said. "Through a bank named Kursk."

Marat looked thoughtful. I heard Kalugin grunt.

"Kursk is owned, through many cutouts, of course, by an oligarch friend of Putin," Marat Rahm said. "I knew Putin. He was in a different section of the KGB but we crossed paths occasionally, when we had mutual interests. I didn't like him, then. And I don't like him now. But he is a very capable man. Everyone knew he was ambitious. A killer at heart, but with brains. And a memory. He never forgets, as some recent assassinations, poisonings and the like outside Russia, attest. The breakup of the Soviet Union was the best thing that could have happened for him. He would have gone far in the old KGB, but not as far as he has now."

The old man smiled.

"I left the KGB after the breakup and went into business for myself and my family, first in Russia and then here. I thought stealing here would be easier. I may have been shortsighted. Putin stayed in Russia and has made billions for himself and his oligarch friends."

"We've done well, Papa," Arman said.

"Oh, I'm not complaining. Even though we've had some problems in America."

He sighed and paused, undoubtedly thinking of his eldest son's murder during the time the Rahms consolidated their American organization.

"But there would have been more blood in Russia unless we went along with Putin. Kursk is a front. Some of its funds will be used to finance criminal activities in America. Activities controlled from Russia. Activities that may very well compete with ours."

I couldn't resist.

"I thought many of your businesses were now legitimate, Mr. Rahm."

"You are teasing, of course. Many, not all. And we have to pay taxes on the legitimate ones."

He must have seen the look on my face.

"Yes, unlike many people, we pay our taxes. But some of our other enterprises are run more informally. Off the books, I think the phrase is."

"The Government sent Capone away for not paying taxes on income he didn't report," I said.

"Capone didn't have our new accountant," Arman said. "He used to work in Hollywood, in the movie business, turning losses into profits."

"Forgive me, Mr. Rahm, but I know you launder your 'informal' cash in your legitimate operations. Aren't you doing what those other Russians are doing?"

"But there is a difference. They are Russians. I am now an American."

Marat Rahm smiled again.

"You might call us financial patriots."

The doorbell rang. Kalugin, who always answered the door, got off the wall and left the room.

"Ah, good," Marat said. "Lunch. I wish you could join us, Alton. Arman, open up a couple of bottles of the Ruffino Ducale and bring some glasses."

Kalugin reappeared, carrying two pizza boxes. He set them on the table and opened them. Arman tilted them toward me, just to rub it in. One was plain, the other had mushrooms and onions. Both thin-crust.

"What's more American than pizza," Marat said.

"I can almost smell it," I said.

"Lee's Tavern," Marat said. "Best pizza in the city."

"I agree with you, Mr. Rahm. But I didn't know Lee's delivered."

"They do to me," he said simply.

He took a slice, and bit it.

"Delicious. This is cruel, I know. But I'm hungry. And I know you can get good pizza in San Francisco."

The old man took a sip of wine and wiped his mouth.

"I do not have to tell you to be careful," he said. "Not after the car bomb. There are billions involved, and politics, as well. There is an old Russian proverb.

'*Ochevidnoye ne vsegda otvet.*'"

"Well, thank you, Mr. Rahm."

I had been hoping for more than a proverb.

"Russian proverbs are usually worthless," he continued, "repeated by old crones with nothing better to do. But this one may apply."

"What does it mean?"

"The obvious is not always the answer."

Marat Rahm picked up another slice, and smiled.

"Oh, by the way, that oligarch that is close to Putin. The one who runs Kursk in Russia, and, I am sure, from Russia. His name is Oleg Kuznetsov. A common name for an uncommon man. A real *golovorez*."

"That means thug," Arman chimed in.

"Gee, I thought it meant sweetheart," I said.

I heard Kalugin chuckle.

"Well, I wish you luck," Marat said. "Kuznetsov and his Kursk people can be very dangerous. If you want, I can put Maks on a plane. The two of you seem to work well together. As I said, our interests may be aligned."

I was tempted. A man who once fell asleep in a dentist chair while getting his teeth cleaned without anesthesia can come in handy in a pinch. But it is hard to keep the body count manageable when Kalugin was around. I also didn't want to discourage anyone from making a move on me. Maks can be very discouraging. And he was keeping an eye on Alice, an idea that looked much better after the car bomb.

"Thank you. Mr. Rahm. I'll keep that in mind in case I need someone to start my car."

"Idi nakhuy yaka," Kalugin said, but not unkindly.

"Don't bother translating that," I said, laughing. "Maks has said it to me many times. We're a little short of yaks out here, though."

Marat Rahm toasted me with his wine.

"By the way, Alton, in case you are wondering, I only wear this sweater when I'm at home eating Italian food. Hides the stains."

CHAPTER 28 - RESEARCH

I believe the Internet, and its spawn, social media sites, have a lot to answer for. Touted as a way to bring people together electronically and almost instantly, they have, in many ways, metastasized the spread of falsehoods and innuendo, not to mention abusive pornography, racism and other societal evils. That being said, internet search engines such as Google and Yahoo have been a boon to private investigators.

If you can't lick 'em, join 'em.

In the days of phone books and shoe leather, in-depth research into the machinations of Russian politics and banking might have taken weeks, even if I figured out how to do it. I'd probably have to interview academics and government bureaucrats, assuming that they would give me the time of day. And if I annoyed the wrong people, I risked being poisoned by some Putin operative. Nowadays, much of the information I needed was only a few computer clicks away. So, I googled.

"Kursk Integrity Bank", "Oleg Kuznetsov" and "Russian Oligarchs" all rated Wikipedia citations, not to mention dozens of articles from Internet journals. Just about all of the latter were critical. But one, a short piece in something called *The Business of Business* caught my eye:

After almost two years of lobbying, Russian banking bigwig Oleg Kuznetsov was recently taken off the U.S. sanctions list. The Treasury Department has notified Congress that Kuznetsov, an oligarch known to be close to Russian President Vladimir Putin, will be free to expand the footprint of his financial holding company, Kursk Integrity Bank.

Kuznetsov was one of seven Russian oligarchs sanctioned in mid-2016 for funding Putin's incursions in Syria and Ukraine. The lifting of sanctions on Kuznetsov required the Treasury to seek a Congressional exemption, through a special resolution, from the Countering America's Adversaries Through Sanctions Act. The resolution was attached as a last-minute rider to a bipartisan bill providing Federal funding for Toys for Tots programs at military bases. The bill was approved, unanimously, just before Christmas.

"No one in Congress would vote against Toys for Tots for the children of men and women in the armed forces during the Christmas season," said Clyde Butcher, an analyst with Mercator Investing, a Burbank-based investment firm. "The bill's sponsors knew that."

Kuznetsov, also suspected of trying to interfere in the American electoral process, has reportedly spent almost $10 million on Washington lobbyists, including several currently under indictment for consorting with a foreign power. And it is suspected of funding various PAC's that give financial support to several key U.S. Senators.

Kuznetsov's bank, Kursk, is informally known as "Putin's piggy bank". But with the sanctions lifted, it is free to expand in the U.S., where it has been making spectacular inroads in California.

"Kursk is eating Wells Fargo's lunch in San

Francisco," Butcher said. "Wells Fargo has had a tough time recovering from that scandal where it opened up thousands of accounts in its customers' names without telling them, just to charge them fees."

Fred Prancy, who runs the financial watchdog site Not Again, America, takes an even more jaundiced view of Kursk.

"The bank has another agenda. A political agenda. Substitute the name Putin for Kursk and it becomes clear."

I then went to the Wikipedia citations. They were more even-handed, and there was a lot of repetitious boiler plate, but it was hard to disguise the animus most contributors felt toward the Russians. I found a couple of photos of Kuznetsov and Putin together, usually at some political or business function. In a shot of Putin in a skimpy bathing suit about to jump into an icy river to prove his manhood, Kuznetsov and some others were in the background, sensibly clothed on a dock.

Further down in the copy, there was a more informal shot at some sort of family gathering. The Kuznetsov family, the caption said. Wife, Svetlana; daughters, Natalia and Tanya; son, Barri. Nice-looking clan, the photo taken a decade earlier, since more-current photos of Oleg Kuznetsov showed him balder and fatter. Svetlana was tall and thin, with high cheekbones, and I guessed that she aged better than her husband. Same with the kids, all tall. The daughters were quite attractive. Oleg might provide the rubles, but his wife provided the genes. Barri Kuznetsov was the only one not smiling. His dour expression detracted from what might have been a handsome face, also marred by a flattish nose. He looked bored. A line in the caption said that Barri Kuznetsov boxed in the Russian equivalent of the Golden Gloves ("Zolotyye Perchatki)".

That probably explained the nose.

I was about to move on when something caught my eye. I enlarged the family photo. I looked closely at the son, Barri. He was the tallest of the bunch, and already sported a receding hairline. But something else caught my eye. Ten years didn't make that much of a difference. I was staring at someone I'd just seen, in real life.

"Son of a bitch."

I remembered something Marat Rahm had said, about Oleg Kuznetsov.

"A common name for an uncommon man."

It didn't make an impression on me then. But now I had a hunch. I closed out Wikipedia and opened Google. I queried "Common Russian Surnames". It turned out that "Kuznetsov is the third most common Russian surname after "Ivanov" and "Smirnov", which I presume was the basis for the vodka named "Smirnoff". I couldn't help but notice that "Popov", another vodka brand, was in fourth place. Russian alcoholism rates being what they are, the apples apparently never fall far from the family trees. Next, I opened Google Translate and plugged in Smith in the English side. Bingo! Kuznetsov popped up in Russian.

Barry Smith was Barri Kuznetsov. Bad wig and flattened nose.

There had been a Russian in the woodpile, hiding

his real identity. A Russian who worked closely with Kevin Allender and was privy to his work but claimed he hardly knew him. A Russian who knew where Annalise Purna lived and parked her car.

It was more than a clue or a coincidence.

With billions at stake, it was motive.

CHAPTER 29 - BERT AND ERNIE

I followed Barri Kuznetsov for a week. It wasn't hard. For the most part, he got to the bank before 9 AM and left around 6. I didn't care if he spotted me, so I wasn't too surreptitious. I mean, I didn't sit down next to him when he went to a restaurant for lunch, but I knew he noticed me once or twice, at a distance. I resisted the temptation to wave, however.

Bert and Ernie had disappeared, and that bothered me somewhat. So, I kept an eye out for a tail. Despite what you read in some detective novels, it's almost impossible to spot a really professional tail. Especially when more than one person is involved. Nowadays, the little old lady walking her cute little yorkie might be part of a surveillance. Everyone has a smart phone glued to their ears. The little old lady could be exchanging muffin recipes with another old biddie, or passing your route off to another contact.

And, of course, with all the electronic doodads that can be secreted on your person or vehicle, people tracking someone can often do so in the comfort of their homes. Or, they can just track someone's smart phone GPS signature.

So, I intermittently turned off my cell, and checked my person and my vehicle for bugs, big and small. Someday I may have to invest in one of those wand things that the people on TV shows wave around to sweep areas for electronic trackers and eavesdropping gadgets.

As for Bert and Ernie, if I couldn't spot those two weirdos, I'd turn in my secret decoder ring. Even in

San Francisco they would stand out as sore thumbs.

Most nights, Barri left work and went to expensive-looking restaurants. I looked through several windows, and once even went inside. Kuznetsov had drinks and dinner with an assortment of people, most of whom looked like business clients or friends. There was a lot of laughter and everyone seemed to be having a grand time. I wasn't having a grand time, and the various kitchen smells — roasted meats, broiled fish, pasta, Indian cuisine — were killing me. I even ordered takeout at one place only to be haughtily told that perhaps I should try a diner.

Since it didn't appear Barri was doing anything I wouldn't have given my right arm to be doing, I went back to the Westin St. Francis and, of course, gorged myself. Thank God for the hotel gym, which I hit every morning before picking up Barri at the bank.

On Friday, Kuznetsov did not immediately go to a restaurant after work. He drove his car, a silver BMW, down a ramp into a garage that was part of a fancy-looking apartment building on a one-way street in Nob Hill.

I sat in my car considering my options. It was Friday. Perhaps he had planned a later dinner. Or, maybe he was taking it easy and was just going to pop something in a microwave or order a pizza, and watch Netflix.

He could be just visiting someone. Just because he punched a keypad to raise the garage gate didn't mean someone hadn't given him the code. I didn't begrudge Barri a fling, but I didn't want to wait all night while he got his ashes hauled. I could have checked his name and address on my smart phone, but I thought it was time to stir things up a bit.

I went into the lobby, where a uniformed concierge behind a desk was monitoring some video screens.

"Can I help you, sir," he said with a smile.

"Does Barry Smith live here?"

"And you are?"

"Just a friend from the bank. We're supposed to go out to dinner and I said I'd pick him up. Can you call his apartment and tell him Miles Archer is here?"

"Certainly, Mr. Archer."

He picked up the phone.

"I wasn't sure this was the right address. I parked up the street. Just tell him I'll pull up front, will you?"

"Of course, sir."

I went to my car, which was actually parked nearby, and drove around the block. Then, I did park up the street next to a fire hydrant, where I had a good view of the lobby and adjacent garage.

Kuznetsov came out of the building and looked around. I was pretty sure he couldn't see me through my car's tinted glass, but I ducked down a bit anyway. Then, he went back in, and probably gave the concierge some grief.

Not a half hour later, Barri's BMW came out of the garage and sped away. I followed.

It was Friday night and rush hour, so it took us a while to get out of the city. I was driving a nondescript car in a sea of cars, so I wasn't worried about being spotted. Even when we got on US 280, a major highway, all I was to Kuznetsov was just another set of headlights.

After about 40 minutes on the highway, he pulled off at an exit that said Emerald Hills. Soon we were winding our way through streets where the houses became further and further apart. There were fewer cars on the road, which made following Kuznetsov's car more difficult, but his taillights were mentally imprinted on my brain and I was able to keep him in sight even when I allowed another car to get between us.

All the same, I almost missed it when he turned up a narrow road that spiraled further up the hills. Now, the large houses were on bigger lots and recessed from the road. It was an expensive neighborhood. I doused my own lights and let the BMW get way ahead of me.

It wouldn't have mattered. The road we were on ended in a small cul-de-sac. There were five houses, two on each side and one in the middle. I watched as Kuznetsov pulled into the driveway of the middle home. I was driving slowly, which was fortunate, since with my headlights doused, I almost plowed into a white van parked in front of the nearest house on the right.

It was very dark but I could see Kuznetsov stop at the beginning of the driveway and get out of his car. His headlights were still on. They went off automatically just as he opened the front door and entered. It was dark inside. In fact, the entire house was unlit.

He shut the door behind him. A light appeared in the transom above the door. Presumably a hall light. Then another in a room to the side. I pulled out from behind the van. As I moved past it, I noticed the lettering on its side: WEST COAST CABLE. I drove to the end of the cul-de-sac and pulled in behind the BMW.

Catching Kuznetsov alone was a bonus. I went to the window of the room, apparently a den, that had been lighted. I peered in. Kuznetsov was at a wet bar pouring himself a drink. It looked like vodka. In the center of the room was a pool table, with balls already racked. I went to the front door and rang. A moment later he opened the door, holding his drink.

"You again!"

His eyes drifted down to the gun I was holding.

"We have to talk, Kuz. Let's go into the den. You can make me a drink."

Kuznetsov backed up and I whirled him around and gave him a gentle push. The rest of the house was still dark. He walked into the den and over to the wet bar. He turned around. And smiled.

That was disconcerting. He didn't seem to be all that concerned about the precariousness of his position. His smile widened. I again noticed how yellow his teeth were.

"Drop the gun!"

Coming from Kuznetsov, the remark would have been hilarious. But it came from behind me. And "ruki vekh!" from off to the side with a different voice explained Kuznetsov's nonchalance.

"He means 'hands up'," he said. "He's fond of old Westerns. But just place the gun on the pool table. That will suffice."

I glanced, slowly, to my right. It was "Bert", holding a large revolver with a silencer. I assumed

"Ernie" was the voice behind me, similarly armed.

I looked at the racked balls. In the movies a man in my position would grab them and in two quick motions fire them into the foreheads of the gunmen, and retrieve his gun and the initiative in one fell swoop. In real life, I would be shot full of many holes.

I gently placed my gun on the table.

"Can we turn on some more lights, now, boss," Bert said. "It was getting creepy in here waiting for you two."

I had been expected.

"Like a spider expects a fly."

"What's that?" Kuznetsov said.

"I was just reflecting on my stupidity," I said.

"Don't be too hard on yourself, Mr. Rhode," he said. "You've managed to learn a lot about my plans."

"You mean your father's, don't you?"

"My father! Ha! Perhaps you don't know as much as I thought. Well, we shall soon find out, shall we not?"

What the hell was he talking about?

Kuznetsov walked up to me and picked up my gun. It was the five-shot .38 revolver I carry when I don't expect real trouble. I should have brought a bazooka. He put the gun in his pocket.

He was standing close enough to me that I thought I saw a chance. His men might not shoot for fear of hitting him. I threw a jab at Kuznetsov's chin, hoping to stun him enough so that I could whirl him around and put him between Bert and Ernie. If I grabbed my gun from his pocket, I might have chance.

He slipped my jab easily, then counter punched me

in the solar plexus. Hard. I doubled over.

"I used to box," he said.

"I know," I gasped, straightening up. "How did you keep that crappy wig on in the ring? Super Glue?"

I thought I heard Ernie chuckle before Kuznetsov put me down with what might have been the best right cross this side of Minsk.

CHAPTER 30 - MORE BASEMENT BLUES

I came to with the help of a bucket of cold water splashed in my face. I shook the haze and droplets from my eyes and everything slowly came into focus. I started to look around but the throbbing pain in my head stopped me. I felt my gorge rise but the nausea soon subsided. I worked my mouth. Nothing broken. Felt around with my tongue. Tasted blood, although I seemed to have all my teeth. But my jaw was sore as hell. I moved my head slowly.

I was in a large, well-lighted room with a cement floor. There were metal cabinets and workbenches along the walls, and a set of stairs heading up. A basement.

One expects a basement to smell, well, like a basement. Musty, perhaps. Moldy, for sure. A finished basement, of course, is really part of the house, with maybe a tile floor, a stove-and-fridge area that growing up was derisively called a "summer kitchen" as a put-down of Italian-Americans by the parents of some of my friends. Funny, the kids, me and my pals, loved going into those finished basements to watch TV, play board games and smell what had been cooked there, and hoped for meatball sandwiches or other such delicacies.

The basement I was now in did not smell like meatballs. It had a stringent, not unpleasant, odor of good disinfectant.

Other than my head, I couldn't move much of anything. I had been in this position before. In a chair. Hands tied behind me. Feet bound. Totally helpless. In my own unfinished basement at home. By an obese Mafia maniac who hated me.

I didn't think Kuznetsov hated me. He just wanted information. Which made my current situation precarious. I was pretty sure I didn't have the information he wanted. Even if I did, I wouldn't tell him. So, I was probably going to be tortured to death for telling the truth. That didn't seem quite fair. It was the *Marathon Man* scenario. The Nazi dentist played by Laurence Oliver kept asking Dustin Hoffman, "Is it safe?" and Hoffman didn't know what the hell he was talking about. Out came the dental drill, sans Novocaine.

Bert and Ernie, the two thugs who had gathered me up, sat smoking and playing chess at a small table on which lay a large toolbox. Russians love chess. I didn't care about their smoking. It seemed a bit out of place to warn them of the danger to their health. It was my health that mattered to me.

I was more worried about the toolbox. Generally speaking, a toolbox in an area where you are about to be interrogated is not a good sign. If it contained a dental drill I was in serious trouble.

'Who is winning?" I said, just to be conversational.

They both looked at me.

"Not you," Ernie said.

"Are you the guys who threw Allender off his balcony and planted the car bomb?"

"Da," Bert said.

"English, Yuri," Ernie chided. "Practice makes perfect."

He looked at me.

"You will have to forgive my partner. He is new to the country. He means 'yes'."

"I got that," I said. "Are you two Muppets planning to throw me off a building, too?"

"That would be impractical," a voice behind me said. "You are in a basement."

The two henchmen thought the remark was hilarious and started laughing. I was less amused. Kuznetsov came around to stand facing me.

"I want to ask you some questions."

"I'll save you the trouble. It's safe."

He looked confused for a second. But then smiled.

"Very good. I saw the movie. I've avoided going to the dentist since."

"I can see that. And your breath could stop a locomotive."

"You are a funny man, Rhode." Kuznetsov's smile had morphed into a sneer. "I didn't bring a dental drill. Although if you don't answer me truthfully, you'll wish I had. What I plan is much worse."

He snapped his fingers and said, 'chair'.

I heard metallic scraping and Bert placed a chair in front of me. He smiled at me and went back to his chess game. Kuznetsov sat. I could tell by the slight bulge and the way his jacket sagged that my gun was still in his right pocket. I filed the information away, although I wasn't sure it would prove useful.

Still, it was a mistake on his part.

"Fill up the bucket," he said.

Ernie got up and I heard a tap screech and the bucket filling.

"That won't be necessary," I said. "I'm wide

awake."

"I know," Kuznetsov said. "It's not for that. It's for the cleanup later."

The disinfectant smell now took on a more sinister and unpleasant meaning. I suspected I was not the first person ever to be tied up in this particular basement. Ernie placed the bucket next to my chair.

"Anything else," Ernie said, a bit impatiently.

He was anxious to get back to his chess game. Either he was losing or had a good move in mind.

"No," Kuznetsov said. He turned to me. "Now, my questions. Hard or easy?"

From the table I heard Ernie say, "Check!"

"Sukin sin!" Burt said. *Son of a bitch.*

Kuznetsov looked annoyed.

"If you two can't be quiet, go upstairs!"

I heard some more chair scraping sounds and both men headed upstairs, with Ernie carefully carrying the chessboard.

"Make sure you close the door," Kuznetsov said.

"Idiots," Kuznetsov murmured. "Now, where were we?"

I was alone in the basement with Kuznetsov. Another mistake.

"You said something about hard or easy," I rasped.

A plan began to form in my mind. I wiggled my hands behind me. I would take a pummeling, but the alternative was worse.

"Yes, do you want this hard or easy?"

"The questions?"

Kuznetsov sighed.

"Your answers."

"And if you get them easy?"

"Then you die easy."

"I don't suppose we could skip the torture and go straight to the dying. Save time."

Kuznetsov shook his head in resignation.

"Where is Annalise?"

I was having a little trouble with the dryness in my mouth, but I managed to say, "Idi nakhuy yaka".

Maks Kalugin would have been proud of me.

Kuznetsov punched me again and I fell over backwards in the chair. The punch, and my head hitting the cement floor momentarily stunned me. When my head cleared, Kuznetsov was standing over me, looking down.

I pretended to be groggier than I was, while I scraped the twine around my wrists against the cement. I wasn't planning to wear through them. But my hands hadn't been bound tightly enough, and the water from my face bath had made them slick.

Another mistake on their part.

Kuznetsov reached down, grabbed my shirt and pulled me upright. He was a strong man. Then he went to the table and brought over the toolbox. He opened it. I was surely projecting, but everything in it looked medieval. Kuznetsov gave it a slight kick, for effect.

"Where is she?"

"Why don't we play 20 questions?"

He casually reached into the toolbox and came out with a medium-sized screwdriver, which he plunged into my right leg above the knee. I screamed.

"Yell all you want," Kuznetsov said. "I had this basement soundproofed. Once the door at the top of the stairs is closed, no one can hear you."

He yanked the screwdriver out. Blood pooled out on my pants leg. I could feel it running down my calf.

"Next time, I'll use a Phillips screwdriver," he said. "Then we will move up to power tools."

"Anything but those powderpuff punches you throw, Barry. Did you fight in the woman's division? I bet you didn't last a round."

Still sitting, he snapped a good jab into my nose. It wasn't enough to rock me all the way back, so I pushed off the ground with my feet. He didn't notice. I managed to bend my neck so that when my back hit the floor I limited the damage to my head. Blood poured out of my nose and my leg, mixing with the water on the floor. Making the twine and my wrists even more slippery. A hell of a trade off, but one that might keep me alive. I scraped my bindings against the concrete floor.

Kuznetsov righted me again. I shook my head and pretended that I was stunned, all the while working my hands looser. Almost there.

One more punch was all I needed.

CHAPTER 31 - CHECKMATE

Kuznetsov reached into the toolbox and came out with a drill. The kind that locks various drill bits into place. He chose one that looked like it would have no trouble punching through bricks. In comparison, a Phillips screwdriver looked pretty good to me.

"Damn," Kuznetsov said.

The drill's cord wouldn't reach the nearest outlet. My reprieve was short-lived. He pulled out an extension cord and walked over to a wall outlet and plugged it in. Then he sat back down and attached the drill. He pressed a button and the drill rumbled to life. Then he shut it off and put it down.

"Last chance, Rhode. Where is she?"

I whispered something.

"What?"

I whispered again, and added a head droop to sell my grogginess. It worked. He leaned forward.

"What?"

I spit in his face. I was taking a hell of a chance. But, then again, I really had no choice. Would he go for the drill, or punch me again?

The boxer in him won. He belted me and I fell back. It was a good shot. I didn't need any help from my feet to crash on my back and arms.

Kuznetsov was so enraged he actually helped my plan by putting a foot on the chair and pushing it. That extra movement scraped the last of the twine binding off my hands. I wasn't home free, but Kuznetsov, cursing too fast in Russian for me to translate, helped me out again. He grabbed me by the shirt and pulled me, and the chair, upright.

I kept my arms behind me until the range was right and then smashed both my fists as hard as I could against his ears. While he was stunned, I reached into his pocket for my gun. Still seated, I leaned back and kicked him in the crotch with my bound feet.

It was a devastating kick, two feet tied together being better than one. It was the kind of thing that could only be done while seated. Remembering Anna's surprise kick to my groin, I actually winced in male solidarity.

Kuznetsov curled up and crashed onto the floor. Now, it was his time to scream.

I hopped, rather inelegantly, over to the tool box, found some sheers that undoubtedly would have been used on me, and cut my feet loose. Kuznetsov was making horrible sounds, rolling on the floor and trying to get to his feet. It was an effort made more difficult because he was holding his balls. I smashed the butt of my gun on the back of his neck. He went down like a stone. He'd be out for a while.

I listened for the door upstairs. Nothing. Thanks to the soundproofing, Bert and Ernie were busy playing chess. I went up the stairs and opened the door.

They saw me at about the same time. Their guns were draped over their respective chairs, and they went for them simultaneously. I shot them each twice in the chest. Bert grunted and fell backwards but Ernie silently pitched forward on the table. Chess pieces flew in every direction.

I checked to be sure both men were dead. They were. I headed back down to the cellar. At the last moment I turned to look at the late Bert and Ernie.

"Checkmate," I said.

Cheesy, I know.

***

Kuznetsov was exactly where I left him, motionless. I wondered if I had hit him too hard. I needed him alive. For one thing, I wanted to know why he had to kill Allender and was still after Anna. For another, without proof he did anything, I'd have a hard time explaining three corpses, two with my ammunition in them.

I dragged him over to "my" chair and trussed him the way I'd been. Except better. Arms bound tightly, each leg tied separately to a chair leg. I wasn't worried about him grabbing for my gun, which was now nestled in the trouser band against my back. I doubted he could see it and I'd tied his bindings just short of inducing gangrene.

The floor was still wet and slick, with a pinkish color, thanks to my blood, which continued to drip steadily from my thigh wound. I went over to a workbench and spied a half-filled bottle of cheap vodka next to an empty bag full of wrappers of recently eaten fast-food hamburgers. There were some clear napkins that I soaked in the vodka and swabbed my leg wound. The burning sensation was actually cathartic. There was also a semi-clean rag on the bench. I soaked that too and wrapped it tight around my thigh. Then I took a large swig of the vodka.

That was also cathartic.

"Pomogite! Pomogite!"

I was so startled I almost dropped the vodka bottle.

That was something I knew Kalugin would never approve. Kuznetsov had come to and was shouting.

"Pomogite! Pomogite!"

Then, he switched to English.

"Help!" Help!"

"Barri. Did you forget about the soundproofing?"

He looked at me.

"My men will check up on me. They will kill you!"

"Not unless they are zombies," I said, reluctantly putting down the vodka.

He looked confused. Then it sank in.

"You killed them!"

I sat down in front of him.

"It seemed the prudent thing to do."

Kuznetsov began struggling against bindings.

"Don't bother," I said. "You were sloppy. I'm not."

"They are too tight. They hurt."

"It's all relative, Barry. In a moment they will hurt less than the rest of you."

CHAPTER 32 - DADDY ISSUES

I was doing a bit of bluffing. But Kuznetsov didn't know that. To him, the playing field was now reversed. He was helpless and his former victim, bruised, bloodied and presumably boiling mad now had the upper hand. In a soundproofed basement, with no help in sight. A look of unbridled fear crossed his face. He swallowed.

"What do you want?"

"You mean other than a left-handed power hitter for the Yankees? Not much, really. Just a few answers."

"You will get nothing out of me."

"Poor choice of words, Barry." I started rummaging around noisily in the toolbox. "Some of these items seem designed to be invasive. Thanks for the box by the way. Saves me the trouble of going to a Home Depot. Looking like I do after your ministrations, I'd probably get arrested."

The reference to the tools and my wounds was intentional. I was pretty sure that with blood clotted in my nose, a swollen eye, a lumpy jaw and a bandaged leg I looked mad enough to seek revenge. I wanted to frighten him even more than he was.

But other than perhaps slapping him around a bit, mostly as payback for turning me into his personal punching bag earlier, I had no intention of torturing him. Where was Maks Kalugin when I needed him? Maks went full-Guantanamo on a redneck killer down South not too long ago. It worked to my advantage then, but I didn't have much stomach for it then, or now.

But Kuznetsov didn't know that.

"I won't talk!"

I lifted the power drill and turned it on. Kuznetsov couldn't take his eyes of the whirring drill bit. I moved it toward his crotch and started whistling "*Dixie*". The "*Song of the Volga Boatman*" would probably have been more appropriate, but "*Dixie*" was the only tune that popped into my head.

Kuznetsov spewed a stream of invective in Russian too fast for my limited vocabulary to keep up.

"Barri, with an 'i' by the way, please stick to English," I said. "Although in the spirit of detente you can scream in Russian."

The drill bit got as far as his zipper, which was as far as I was willing to go. The whirring sound changed as metal hit metal. I was getting nervous. The drill was heavy. I didn't want my hand to slip.

Kuznetsov folded like a Yugo in a head-on crash.

"I'll talk! I'll talk! Are you crazy! I'll tell you everything!"

In perfect English. I turned off the drill. I couldn't help but wonder how many holes Kuznetsov would have drilled into me when he asked me questions for which I had no answers.

"I'll start with an easy one. Why did you kill Kevin Allender?"

"The fool wanted to go public with his idea for Golden Gate."

"So? What was the big deal?"

"So, it was a brilliant concept. But he thought the tree huggers and companies trying to project a socially conscious image would welcome the system."

"The system being a closed blockchain universe with its own cryptocurrency dedicated to doing good and saving the planet," I said.

Kuznetsov stared at me.

"I had a good teacher," I explained. "But what did you care?"

Before he could answer, it hit me.

"You wanted Golden Gate for yourself."

He nodded.

"Keep going, Barri."

He hesitated and I pressed the trigger on the drill, which started whirring.

"We were going to patent Golden Gate. No one else could use the system. Kursk would have been able to draw investors from everywhere. Environmental groups, major corporation, philanthropists, the people in the streets. They would have thrown money at us."

"How can you patent an idea?"

"You can't. But it would take time for the lawyers to figure it out. And any potential competitors would hesitate to create the correct digital architecture and mine the cryptocurrency. We already had Allender's architecture and have been mining for months."

"And all this was worth killing two people?"

"Golden Gate is worth billions."

"God, you ex-Commies make the best capitalists. Your old man must be very proud of you."

"My father? What does he have to do with this?"

"He runs Kursk."

Kuznetsov sneered.

"My father is a Putin puppet. All he wants is a

bank in America where he can launder money for the right politicians. We never got along. He thought I was a wastrel. I became an amateur boxer just to impress him. And I was good! But he thought I was frivolous. That's why he sent me here. To straighten me out. He wouldn't understand Golden Gate. And even if he did, he'd probably just reinvest the money, or siphon some of it back to Putin. Even your retarded banking authorities or Securities and Exchange Commission might eventually catch on. I planned on being long gone before that happens, or before someone else copies the system."

Another mental light bulb flashed on.

"You were going to embezzle the money!"

Kuznetsov smiled. Despite his predicament, talking about his scheme delighted him.

"Embezzlement is such a nasty term. I've been 'borrowing' money from the bank. Mining bitcoins is expensive. Once I get Golden Gate up and running, I'll pay it all back."

His smile became expansive.

"Of course, then I'd turn my billions of crypto holdings into real cash."

"Kursk's cash, of course."

"But, of course. A few keystrokes and that cash is transferred out of the country."

"And then you disappear, as well."

"It would be the prudent thing to do."

"They'd catch you."

"Please. The legitimate banks, if you want to call them that, lose billions all the time. No one even goes to jail in this country. In Russia, you might, unless you were a friend of Putin. In China, they'd probably shoot you in the head, and make your family pay for the bullet. And I planned to add to the confusion with the bitcoins. By the time anyone figured out what happened, I'd be long gone, with a bunch of American lawyers muddying the waters for a decade."

Kuznetsov laughed harshly.

"I've already made inquiries. I'd have to pay them real money, of course, not crypto. Those bloodsuckers insisted. But it would be worth it. In a few years there will be another huge financial scandal that your taxpayers will be forced to underwrite and I'd be a footnote, if that. Study your history, my friend. The crooks of the 80's and 90's are now respectable philanthropists. More recent crooks were asked to fix the system they themselves fucked up. Some of them are still in power in Washington and Wall Street."

"I guess you weren't planning to go back to Russia."

"God forbid! Too cold. Someplace warm, with lusty women, a government I could bribe and a non-extradition treaty."

"Cuba, maybe? Or Venezuela?"

"Are you insane? I wouldn't trust the Communists with my money!"

I would have laughed at that line, but my face and jaw were aching.

"I imagine daddy would have been pissed."

"Fuck him. His whoring killed my mother. But listen, Rhode, you have the upper hand now. But if you are willing to let bygones be bygones, my plan can still work. I'll cut you in. The girl, too, if you want.

You'll be rich beyond your wildest dreams."

"I have some pretty wild dreams."

"They can all come true. All you have to do is throw in with me."

"You killed Kevin Allender."

"What's he to you?"

"My love's ex-husband."

Barri brightened.

"So, what's the problem? I did you both a favor."

I smiled. It hurt a bit, but I couldn't help it. His logic, to him at least, was inescapable.

CHAPTER 33 - PILLOW TALK

I heard a loud knock on the door at the top of the cellar stairs. A gleam of hope appeared in Kuznetsov's eyes.

I took my gun out and pointed it at his nose.

"One peep out of you and I'll kill you."

That wasn't a bluff. But just to make sure he kept quiet, I went over to the table and grabbed a roll of duct tape and sealed his lips. Then, I crept up the stairs and slowly peered into the kitchen.

A well-dressed Chinese man, who looked very familiar, was examining the bodies at the kitchen table. He looked up at me. His eyes drifted to the gun I pointed at him.

"You can put that away, Alton. I don't think you want to shoot me. Especially since I think we are on the same side."

Despite the fact that he was now wearing a blue suit, I now recognized him.

Jian Chen. Sandra Wong's date.

I noticed two other Chinese men standing in opposite doorways. Both had automatic pistols pointing at me.

"There are two more out in the van," Chen said.

He nodded at the men, and they lowered their guns. So did I.

"The white van," I said. "West Coast Cable."

"Very observant, Alton. We were sitting in listening to what was going on. Cable vans are ubiquitous. You can park them anywhere. Even out here in the boondocks. No one pays attention to the name either, which is phony, of course."

"Apparently, I wasn't observant enough. I wound up trussed in the basement about to be turned into a woodworking project. You might have come in a lot sooner."

"I'm sorry about that, Alton. We didn't put bugs everywhere. This is Kuznetsov's weekend retreat and the neighborhood is isolated. We concentrated on his phones and the rooms where we thought he might do business. There was no bug in the basement. But when we heard shots, we came in. Through the back. It took a few minutes to check all the rooms. I had just gotten to the kitchen. From the looks of these two, I assumed you had things under control. But I didn't know what we might walk into if we just went down the stairs. That would be iffy, tactically. You might shoot first and ask questions later. So, I knocked."

He pointed at the corpses.

"Nice going, by the way. Two shots each. Close together."

"Thanks, I think. I've had some practice. What I lack in caution I've often had to make up in accuracy."

Chen laughed.

There were four chairs around the kitchen table. Two had blood pooling under them. Chen pulled two of the other chairs away from the table and sat in one. He patted the other.

"Sit, Alton. We have much to talk about. By the way, where is Kuznetsov? Dead?"

"No. Tied up in the basement."

"From your appearance, it appears he wasn't easy to subdue. I knew he was a boxer, Alton, but you look like you fought a lion."

I told Chen what had transpired. He shook his head and smiled.

"It seems everything I found out about you is true."

"You investigated me?"

"Just on Google. Amazing what you can learn with a few mouse clicks. The Internet may put me out of business soon. You, too."

He said something in Chinese to one of his men, who headed down the stairs.

"What is he going to do?"

"Just keep an eye on him."

"He's barely able to move."

"Better safe than sorry," Chen said, pointing at the late Bert and Ernie. "You are certainly proof of that."

"I take it you are not a Cultural Attaché."

"Assistant Cultural Attaché. But I have other duties."

"Just what do they call the Chinese Secret Service?"

"Just google it."

I had to laugh. Despite all the guns in the room, and the noxious odors and various fluids emanating from Bert and Ernie's settling corpses, my situation didn't seem particularly precarious.

"So, Alton, what brought you to San Francisco."

What the hell? Everyone seemed to have a finger in the pie, so I decided to tell him.

"Try to keep up," I said.

"Amazing," he said, when I finished. "What a tangled web we weave. Well, if it makes a difference, it became personal to me, as well."

"Sandy. Your girlfriend?"

Chen smiled wistfully.

"No. Sandra Wong was a wonderful girl, but a bit young for me. And not my cup of sexual tea."

I wondered what he meant by that.

"Besides, I am happily married. Sandra was one of our best agents."

"She was spying on Anna."

"In a manner of speaking. Really, just keeping an eye on her. Trying to figure out what Kuznetsov was up to. She and Anna really were friends, in a way. I never thought it would get her killed. Putin and his oligarch friends may be ruthless, but killing an American citizen who is not a direct threat would be counterproductive. Why bother when he can hack your elections? No, it never occurred to me that Kuznetsov was a lone wolf, scheming on his own."

Chen looked genuinely sad.

"I should have considered it. Sandra might be alive."

"If it's any consolation, I missed it too. I told Kuznetsov that ex-Commies make the best capitalists."

Chen smiled wanly.

"What else did you tell him?"

"Nothing. I didn't know anything he didn't already know."

"What about Anna's whereabouts?"

"I really don't know. He didn't believe me."

Chen sighed.

"Then you were assuredly in for a very unpleasant time in the basement. We followed the trail as far as

Orlando. But then it dried up. Wherever she went to ground, she was untraceable."

If the Chinese Secret Service was stumped, I wondered just where Rahm's men had stashed her after she landed in Florida.

"Clever of you to switch airline terminals, by the way."

"Thanks. It wasn't meant to fool you. Just the car bombers."

"Well, no matter. We just wanted to keep an eye on her. Perhaps find out who set the bomb. She's safe, now."

"What about Golden Gate?"

"Sounds like a wonderful idea. Tell Anna to pursue it. Just not with Kursk. If she needs funding, I may be able to put her in touch with some Chinese investors."

"And what about me?"

"First, we get you to a hospital. Patch you up. Then I presume you will fill Inspector Lin in on everything. Just make sure to blame the bank for everything."

"He told me that someone above his pay grade scotched the investigation."

Chen smiled, enigmatically.

"That was you," I said.

"Not directly," Chen said. "Remember, I am a mere Assistant Cultural Attaché. But the consulate has powerful friends in the Chinese community."

"I presume you want me to keep you out of it."

Chen shrugged.

"I'd prefer it. But no matter. I doubt anyone would believe you without proof. And even if someone suspects you are telling the truth, the media and the government will make your life miserable. I'm sure you have better things to do."

He smiled.

"It might even screw up your wedding plans."

"How the hell did you know about that?"

"Anna told Sandra. Girl talk. Actually, what you Americans call pillow talk. They were occasionally more than mere friends. Miss Purna has quite a libido."

To put it mildly, I thought to myself. The man in the basement shouted something in Chinese. Chen replied in kind.

"Wonderful. Kuznetsov has apparently pissed himself," Chen explained. "More cleanup."

"Speaking of that, what about the two stiffs in this kitchen?"

Now Chen's smile was indulgent.

"We know what to do with bodies," he said.

"And Kuznetsov? Are you going to kill him?"

Chen smiled.

"This isn't a Bourne movie. We are not animals, Alton. Besides, he is still useful. I expect he will go in a diplomatic bag to China. Figure of speech. It's not literally a bag, mind you."

"You would kidnap the son of a Russian oligarch who is close to Putin?"

"Kidnap is such a nasty word. 'Borrow' is more like it. Kuznetsov will be a nice bargaining chip with the Russians, if they even want him back. He was planning to cheat Mother Russia, after all."

"And if they don't want him back?"

"Then, after we get everything from him that we can, we'll probably send him to Russia anyway. The GRU will know what to do with him."

"What about his father? He's very close to Putin."

"Oleg? He will be in an awkward position. Putin is former KGB, which is now the GRU. The Russians are hard people. You know the famous Russian story? If Oleg wants to protect his influence and the rest of his family, he may have to throw his son to the wolves off the sled."

Chen smiled.

"And, of course, we will also let him know his son was going to cheat him, too."

The conversation was bordering on surreal. Some people in the United States were concerned about undocumented immigrants. It occurred to me that the country was awash in foreign operatives, some with diplomatic immunity.

I had come to San Francisco to investigate the apparent suicide of Kevin Allender and put Alice's mind at ease. Now I was involved in the financial equivalent of World War III.

One thing was for sure, Barri Kuznetsov's future was very bleak.

He was probably better off in the basement.

***

Chen was as good as his word.

He drove me in my car to an emergency room, leaving his men behind to handle Kuznetsov and clean up the mess I'd created. He even stood by while a curious ER doctor patched me up.

"What the hell happened to you?" the doc asked

between stitches.

"Martial arts," Chen said. "He trains at my gym."

"You should see the other guy," I said.

"Not a scratch on him," Chen said, smiling broadly.

Just what I needed. A Chinese spook with a sense of humor.

On the way to my hotel, we got our stories straight. When we pulled up to the St. Francis, a valet took my rental. Like everyone in the vicinity of the hotel entrance he looked at my face. I didn't care. All I wanted to do was to find a hard drink and a soft bed.

"Remember, that doctor told you not to drink with those pills he gave you for the pain," Chen said.

"Thanks, mom."

He laughed and signaled to a taxi waiting at the cab stand. He shook my hand.

"Best to Annalise," he said, and left.

I went to my room, opened the mini bar and washed down my pain pills with a scotch.

CHAPTER 34 - THE LAST PLACE

I flew to Florida again. I was spending so much time in the Sunshine State I'd probably have to declare residency for the I.R.S.

But this time I wasn't going to Tampa. That, for obvious reasons, was the last place I'd want to stash Anna for safekeeping. But when I called Arman Rahm again to tell him that she could come out of hiding, I was surprised to discover that she was still in Florida, an hour from Orlando by car.

"I would have thought you would have found someplace safer, perhaps even out of the country."

"Do I detect some sort of recrimination, Alton? Do you perhaps think we don't know how to hide people? I know you once found someone in witness protection, in Florida of all places, but even you could not find Anna this time."

"It's bad form to bring that up, Arman."

I wanted to remind Rahm that I was his stalking horse and Kalugin promptly killed the man I'd found.

"Ok. We're even on the insults, Alton. When you see Anna, I'll let you judge just how safe she was. Some people might argue that she is *out* of the country."

Arman would say no more, other than to tell me to take a redeye to West Palm Beach, where he would meet me.

"West Palm Beach? You're coming down from New York?"

"No," Arman said, "I'm already in Florida. Stuart. On the East Coast. But the Orlando airport is a zoo. I'll pick you up in West Palm. It's close to where I am and more convenient. Text me your flight. But no more questions. I'm busy."

***

Maks Kalugin greeted me warmly when I got off the plane at the West Palm Beach International Airport at about noon. That's to say he nodded his head. I followed him out to the curb, where a powder-blue Bentley was idling with Arman and Marat Rahm in the back seat.

A security guard who was annoying other standing cars left the Bentley alone. In fact, he kept smiling at the Rahms as he maneuvered other cars around the Bentley.

I got in the back and sat across from the Rahms. There was a picnic basket on the seat next to me.

"Nice to see you again, Alton," Marat said.

"Good to see you, too, Mr. Rahm. You are looking well."

It was true. The old reprobate had a healthy glow for a man who many assumed was near death a few years earlier.

"Thank you. The Florida sun has done wonders. I like to stay at the Old Colorado Inn. Wonderful place. Really a compound of historical homes, each one more charming than another. Great restaurants. I am even walking all over Stuart, especially its lovely boardwalk along the St. Lucie River. I plan on outliving my new urologist."

I looked at his son.

"We are buying a lot of property near Stuart, in Martin County," Arman explained. "Golf courses and clubs especially. The area has not been discovered yet by the South Americans and the Russian oligarchs."

"When did you get a Bentley, Arman? I thought you were a Mercedes man."

"I am. But someone who owed me money down here offered it in payment. He'd had a bad run of luck in the Miccosukee casino outside Miami. The car didn't cover what he owed me, but what the hell? I guess I'm getting soft."

"Miccosukee?"

"A tribe that's an offshoot of the Seminole Nation. They split away and got their own casino. Sometimes I wish I was an Indian."

"Native American."

"Whatever."

"Your so-called Native-Americans originally came from Siberia, crossing the land bridge that existed between Russia and Alaska," Kalugin said over his shoulder from the driver's seat. "We could do a DNA test like that woman senator. Might have enough DNA to open a casino."

We stared at him.

"I read the Siberia stuff in National Geographic," Maks said, picking up the iconic magazine from the seat next to him.

Maks Kalugin, Renaissance assassin.

"I still prefer a Mercedes," Marat said, with just a hint of reproach.

"Me, too," Maks added.

Arman shook his head and rolled down his window as the Bentley pulled away.

"Thanks, Fred," he said to the security guard.

"No problem, Mr. Rahm," the man replied, holding up a hand to stop traffic for us.

Arman looked at me.

"I use this airport a lot. Everyone knows me."

"Especially at Christmas, I imagine," I said.

"There's that."

"Is a Bentley practical, Arman? I mean, the trunk only looks big enough for one body."

Even Kalugin laughed.

"I'm glad to see that a black eye and stitches hasn't impaired your sense of humor," his father said.

"I guess the sunglasses don't help that much."

"With a shiner like that, you'd need a lampshade," Arman said. "And what's with the limp?"

"Guy stuck a screwdriver in my leg."

"Ouch!"

"Could have been worse. The next step was a power drill."

"Tell us everything," Marat said. "We have plenty of time before we get to the Villages."

"The Villages?"

"You've heard of it? The big retirement community about an hour west of Orlando?"

"Yes. But why are we going there?"

"Because that is where we put Anna. We have friends there, and it's the last place anyone would look. It's across the state, but we have a few stops to make along the way. Make yourself comfortable."

Arman pushed a button on a console that separated our seats and a small mini-bar rose up. It contained an assortment of liquors, juices and soft drinks, as well as a container of ice and glasses.

"We have some sandwiches and other snacks, cheese, caviar and such. Just the basics. You must be hungry."

I was. We ate. It was my first lunch in a Bentley. I stuck to wine, but it still made me sleepy. My recent trials were catching up with me.

I started to tell them what had transpired out West, but I kept yawning.

"Take a nap," Arman said. "You look all in."

"Yes," his father said. "You can finish your story later."

"Good idea," I said, and promptly fell asleep.

CHAPTER 35 - OKAHUMPKA

I awoke with a start. The windows in the car were again down. The smell of oranges had been replaced by another agricultural odor. It wasn't unpleasant, but I couldn't place it.

"You've been out for almost three hours," Arman said.

"What's that smell?"

"Tomatoes."

I looked out the windows. Hundreds of farmworkers were toiling in the fields on both sides of the road, amid farm machinery and trucks, some of which were filled to the brim with green and red tomatoes. It looked like backbreaking labor. Many of those workers, I knew, were undocumented immigrants. I'd read somewhere that agriculture was one of the American industries that would collapse without illegals. I suspected that I.C.E., like most Americans, stayed out of the fields during harvest season.

And I wondered what tomato pickers thought about the smell of tomatoes.

"Do you want the windows up?" Marat Rahm inquired.

"No. It's fine."

"I love driving around Florida," he said. "Did you know that 40 percent of all the winter tomatoes in the United States are cultivated in this state? Of course, nothing can beat a New Jersey summer tomato for taste, but that is pretty impressive."

"I didn't know you were so interested in Florida,

Mr. Rahm."

"I have many good memories of the place."

"Better than Alton's, I'd guess," Arman Rahm said dryly.

There was a muffled laugh from Kalugin in the front seat.

"Oh, yes," Marat said. "The Capriati incident. Forgive me."

"Water over the dam," I said.

"I seem to recall that had something to do with oranges," Arman said.

"Just shut up, will you," I said.

But we all laughed.

"Anyway," Marat continued, "Florida is such an interesting state. The tomato, orange and sugar interests pour fertilizer into the watershed, particularly Lake Okeechobee, which creates a problem for the tourist industry. Red tide, green algae and the like. Then there are the golf courses, and their fertilizers. Politically, the warring factions, Cuban expatriates, rednecks, the sugar cane lobby, millions of conservative senior citizens and a more progressive middle class all make for a volatile electorate that decides the Presidency and the control of the Senate. Florida is the Poland of America. Everyone wants a piece of it."

"You, too?"

"Yes. The state's problems, which include the occasional hurricane and a million alligators, present a buying opportunity. We have our fingers in many pies. Nursing homes, of course, just like back in the Northeast, but also farmland, cattle ranches and housing developments."

"I thought you've told me you didn't want to be landlocked."

"As a general rule, Russians prefer to be near the sea. That's why Stalin's gulags were so onerous, among other things of course. But that doesn't mean we don't like land as an investment. Especially in Florida, which is a peninsula. You are never too far from the water in this state."

He smiled.

"And with global warming, some of our properties may soon be beach front."

"How far to The Villages?"

"It's about an hour away. But we have to make one more stop."

"One more?"

"You slept through two. Farms that I own. We didn't want to wake you."

"What's the next stop?"

"Okahumpka state prison."

"Were we speeding?"

He laughed. We turned off the road and a few minutes later passed a sign that said: Okahumpka Correctional Institution.

"We have to visit someone," Arman said. "My father and I are the only ones on the visitor's list. But you and Maks also have to sign in. Then you can stay in the car or the visitors center."

"Car," Maks said, adamantly.

"He hates prisons," Marat said.

"I do, too," I said, "but probably not for the same reason. I'll stay in the car. Who are you visiting?"

"One of my former accountants," Marat said. "Mel Saperstein."

"Cook-the-Books Saperstein?" I said.

"An unfortunate nickname," Marat Rahm said. "A very talented accountant. Not as good as our new man, but quite imaginative in his own way."

"I didn't know he was in stir."

"We kept it quiet," Arman interjected. "And he knows how to keep everything quiet."

"How much time did he get?"

"Ten years," Arman said. "He has served two, and will be out in two, for good behavior."

"What's he doing in a state prison? I would have thought the Feds had jurisdiction over tax fraud."

"He was in Florida working on one of our casino deals," Marat Rahm explained, "and fell in love with a cocktail waitress. Imagine, a man of his age." He shrugged. "Oh well, it happens. The heart wants what it wants. Woody Allen was right about that. Anyway, he shot her husband."

"Dead?"

"No," Arman said. "Just wounded. That's why he only got 10 years. The Feds wanted him to roll on us on the accounting side. But Mel is a stand-up guy."

Which meant he kept his mouth shut.

"I thought you told me you paid your taxes."

"I also said we were good Americans," Marat Rahm said with a smile. "That means we avoid some of them. Legally, of course. Well, here we are."

Okahumpka was obviously a medium-security facility. No guard towers surrounded the mix of barbed wire and fencing that enclosed half a dozen two-story red-brick buildings. I spotted several ball fields and even some tennis courts.

"Whistler's mother could break out of this place," I said, as we approached the front gatehouse, where two guards came out and looked us over. Both had sidearms.

"If you get sent here, just thank your lucky stars," Arman said. "Hardly anyone does a full stretch and you'd be nuts to escape. Although Florida in the summer is no picnic, especially inland."

After an inspection of I.D.'s and the Rahm visitors' passes, we were directed to a reception center. I got out of the Bentley to stretch my legs. Maks opened the trunk. He pulled out two suitcases.

"You're right," he said, smiling. "Not big enough for more than one body."

I was becoming a bad influence on Kalugin. He was developing a sense of humor. I lifted one of the suitcases. It was very heavy.

"What's in these suitcases?"

"Books."

I looked at Arman Rahm.

"Security is tighter inside," he said. "They will check what's in the suitcases and I'll be searched, of course. But I've arranged to bring Mel the latest accounting books as well as some course material for his classes. The warden approves. Mel teaches accounting to inmates. In fact, he started the accounting curriculum here. There are a few other inmates here who have cooked books for major corporations or run complicated financial frauds. They are Mel's assistants."

"Crooked accountants teaching accounting to prisoners. We're going to need more prisons."

Both Rahms smiled.

"Hopefully, most of them will go straight," Marat said. "But at the very least, none will be unemployable."

Arman took the suitcases and he and his father went into the building. Maks and I got back into the car.

"You people also stole Alaska," Kalugin said.

"Read your damn magazine," I said.

***

An hour later we were again on the road.

"Mel sends his regards, Maks," Arman said.

I bet he did. Had not Mel been such a standup guy, I was pretty sure the Rahms would have sent Maks to make him permanently horizontal.

"Now, Alton," Marat Rahm said, "what else happened in San Francisco."

I told them. For the most part, other than a few Kalugin grunts when I hit some highlights, both men remained silent. When I got to the screwdriver, Kalugin did opine, "you should stay out of basements."

When I finished, Marat Rahm told his son to roll down a window. The pleasing smell of oranges wafted into the Bentley.

"What does your Alice think about this?"

"I haven't spoken to her about all of it yet, Mr. Rahm. I imagine she will be sad."

"Will you tell her everything?"

"We don't keep secrets from each other."

"Even Anna's, how shall I put it, sexual urges?"

"I may dance around that a bit."

"You could tell her you gave in," Arman said. "From what you told me about Anna, that would explain your injuries."

I laughed.

"What will the San Francisco authorities do about Allender's murder and the car bombing?"

"I called the cop out there who caught the Allender murder and gave him the short version. Told him that I thought his superiors wouldn't stand in his way anymore."

"What did he say about that?"

"Said he'd already been given the green light. Suggested that I might not want to visit San Francisco again any time soon."

"That Chink spy works fast."

"Yes. Chen will steer everything back to the Kursk bank. The scandal will keep the media busy for months. Funny thing is, Oleg Kuznetsov didn't know what his son was doing. But it won't matter. The bank will take the fall."

"The Chinese can be formidable," Marat Rahm said. "Both Russia and America will have their hands full in this century."

"From what you told me earlier about the Russian kleptocracy and the banking system, and now this, about the Chinese," I said, "makes me very afraid for the future of America."

"All is not lost," the old man said, patting my knee. "Don't give up on this country just yet. If you fix the political system, you have a fighting chance."

He paused.

"But I'm still buying real estate."

CHAPTER 36 – THE VILLAGES

The Villages was nothing like I expected.

Once off the main highway, we entered a realm of tree-lined twisting roads and traffic circles. These roundabouts were made more challenging because there seemed to be golf carts at many of the crossings.

"Drive carefully, Maks," Marat Rahm ordered.

Occasionally, we drove under a narrow bridge and I could see golf carts moving across above us. We passed plenty of courses but none of the carts had golf clubs on them. Before I could ask, Arman explained.

"Just about every home in The Villages comes with a golf cart. And if one doesn't come with the home, you buy one. It's the main way of getting around in and between communities. Some people have two or three."

I chuckled.

"What's so funny?"

"I was involved in a slow-speed chase in a golf cart on Bald Head Island not too long ago. I think a turtle passed me. I'll tell you about it someday."

At one roundabout we stopped for a cart that had been decked out to look like a small yacht.

"That one probably cost five figures," Arman said. "Some of them come with bars and liquor cabinets."

Every half mile or so we passed a shopping center. All seemed to be busy.

"The Villages is the fastest-growing American city," Marat Rahm said. "More than 100,000 people live in 17 separate communities. Very conservative politically, always complaining about welfare and illegals, without whom they'd probably starve. And you'd better not tamper with their Social Security and Medicare."

"My father, the liberal," Arman teased.

"If I might continue," Marat said, "the people here have their own newspaper, plenty of schools, concert halls, movie theaters, libraries, archery ranges, social clubs, supermarkets, specialty food stores, golf courses, restaurants, hospitals, of course, you name it. Everything an aging population needs. Ah, here we are."

We left a main road and entered a community of modest ranch homes. All had attached garages; many had the ubiquitous golf carts parked in the driveways.

"Hacienda Hills," Marat explained.

We turned onto Amelia Street and pulled into the driveway of the third house on the left. The garage door was open. I could see an older man tinkering at a tool bench. I didn't see a golf cart. As we got out of the Bentley, Marat put his hand on my arm.

"We told Annalise that she was now safe," he said. "But she doesn't know much more than that."

The man in the garage walked over to us, beaming.

"Marat! So good to see you!"

The man embraced the elder Rahm. Then, he clapped Arman on the back and exchanged a knowing nod with Kalugin. The man came over to me, and we shook.

"You must be the fellow Anna told us about."

He glanced at my face but didn't say anything. I got the impression he was used to battered visitors. He also had a visage that had apparently met a few fists.

"Alton, this is Sean Kiernan," Arman said. "He and his wife, Peggy, have been looking after Anna."

"They are thick as thieves, those two" Kiernan said. "Went shopping. Should be back any minute. Come on inside and let's all have a drink.'

We were about to do that when a golf cart pulled up, as if on cue.

"Ah, here they are," he said.

Anna jumped out of the cart.

"Alton!"

She ran over to me and literally jumped in my arms. She gave me a big kiss, which lingered.

"Get a room," Arman muttered under his breath.

I broke the embrace and looked at Kalugin, who stared at us. I heard the rustle of grocery bags. Maks went over to take the bags from Peggy Kiernan. Unencumbered, she gave kisses to the Rahms.

"You will stay for dinner, won't you?"

"No thank you, Peggy," Marat said. "We have a reservation at the Grill. You know how I like the early-bird specials." He winked at us. "Besides, we have a lot to talk about with Annalise. Private. You understand. But I wouldn't mind stopping by tomorrow for one of your famous breakfasts, if that is all right."

"Of course. I even have some soda bread. I made it today. Anna helped me."

***

The drive to the restaurant took us about 10 minutes. Anna sat next to me and held my hand. Other than cutting her hair, she had not changed her appearance.

"The Kiernans took Anna in, at our request," Arman said. "They once worked for us, in various capacities. Several of our former employees live in The Villages. We buy the houses, which are theirs to keep. No strings attached. Nothing ostentatious, of course. Most of our friends like to keep a low profile. Occasionally, we ask them to put someone up for a short period. No one here notices a visitor. Just about everyone has children and grandkids visiting."

"Sean and Peggy introduced me as their granddaughter," Anna said. "I even went line dancing with them last week. They are super nice."

I heard Kalugin grunt at that last remark. Then, he pulled the Bentley into a space marked "Reserved".

I looked at the sign above the entrance: THE GROUPER GRILL.

"We own it," Arman explained. "It's part of a chain concept we are developing. Prices are a little upscale, but the food is first-rate and the portions huge. In Florida, many seniors take half their lunch or dinner when they leave, and get another meal out of it, so it still fits most budgets. We even give them a free dessert to take home with every entrée when they depart."

"Doesn't that cut into your dessert business while they are in the restaurant?"

"Not as much as you'd think. Many people don't like to eat dessert in public. They want it to look like they are being sensible, or dieting. But once they are behind their own doors, they pig out. And in each little dessert box, there is a flyer and coupon for our wines."

CHAPTER 37 - NEW PARTNER

When we entered, a well-dressed man greeted the Rahms warmly and led us to a private room in the rear of the Grouper Grill. It was obviously used for larger gatherings. The five of us sat at the end of a long rectangular table that had already been set.

"Conrad," Arman Rahm said to the man, who was obviously the restaurant manager, "bring us the best seafood you have to offer and wines that are appropriate. But close the door on your way out and make sure someone knocks when the food comes."

"Yes, Mr, Rahm. I don't think you will be disappointed."

That was for sure.

Once he left, all eyes turned to me.

"Anna, there is something I have to tell you about Sandy Wong," I said.

"Did you find out who killed her?"

"Yes."

"Have they been arrested?"

Both Rahms smiled.

"They are both dead."

Kalugin, a man of few words but many grunts, made a sound of what I assumed was approval.

Anna nodded her head.

"Did you kill them?"

"Yes."

"Are you in trouble?"

"No. But there is more to this. A lot more. Just sit there and listen."

For the next 10 minutes I explained, as best I

could, about Barri Kuznetsov, his plans to steal the Golden Gate system and scam Kursk, Allender's murder and the attempt on her life. And then I told her about Jian Chen and Sandra Wong.

That stunned her.

"I thought Sandy was my best friend. And all the time she was spying on me."

"Anna, one doesn't preclude the other. I think Sandy genuinely liked you. Sure, the Chinese were interested in what you and Allender developed and were suspicious of the Russians. But they didn't know that Kuznetsov was working on his own and was ready to betray, and murder, anyone who got in his way. If Sandy suspected that, she probably would have tried to protect you, both as a friend and a potential asset. Not knowing got her killed."

"What do I do now? We were counting on Kursk to back Golden Gate financially."

"I think you can assume Kursk won't be able to back anything. The Chinese will make sure that the bank is tainted by what Kuznetsov did. No one will believe his father isn't involved. Hell, between the Wells Fargo scandals and Kursk, people in San Francisco will be putting their money under their mattresses."

"So, Golden Gate is effectively dead."

"Not necessarily. Chen said that he could put you in touch with investors."

"I'm supposed to trust the Chinese now?"

"There is another alternative," Marat Rahm interjected.

Anna and I both looked at him.

"My family has access to sufficient funds," he said.

"But you are Russian crooks," Anna blurted.

Both Rahms laughed.

"I'm sorry for that," she said. "I know I owe you a lot. My life, actually."

"You have no obligation to us," Arman Rahm said. "We protected you as a favor to Alton. But as we have explained to him, we are thoroughly Americanized crooks, so to speak, and are always looking for legitimate outlets for our gains, not all of which are ill-gotten. An investment in Golden gate allows us to stick a finger in the eye of both Putin and the Chinese."

Anna looked at me.

"What do you think?"

"Their word is good. And their money is probably cleaner than many of the corporations that will participate in Golden Gate to burnish their image."

There was a knock at the door. Kalugin got up and opened it. Two waiters, warily glancing at Maks, brought in four bottles of wine in two ice buckets and five steaming bowls of lobster bisque. I recognized the labels on the wine bottles. They were probably two of the best Chardonnays and Sauvignon Blancs in the restaurant's cellar.

"Why don't we start with the Chardonnay first," Arman said. "It will go better with the bisque."

"My son, the gourmet," Marat said dryly, nodding at the waiters.

"I learned much from our vintners," Arman said.

He saw the look I gave him.

"As my father said on the ride here, we have fingers in many pies."

The waiters opened all the bottles and poured some Chardonnay into Arman's glass.

He twirled the wine in the glass, took a sip and smiled at the waiters, and they filled everyone's glasses. They eyed Maks on the way out, as well.

The wine was excellent and we started our meal.

"We can wait for the dust to settle from the Kursk scandal," Arman said. "In the meantime, if you agree, we can start the process of mining proprietary bitcoins."

"It's not an easy process," Anna said. "You will need more than money. You will need warehouse space and access to cheap electricity."

"Both of which we have," Arman said. "In Oregon. Along the Willamette River, where hydroelectric power is readily available and inexpensive. We have plenty of land there, mostly devoted to raising grapes for the excellent Pinot Noir we produce, but there is no reason some of it can't be used for bitcoin mining."

I could tell Anna was impressed.

"I would like to think all of this over," she said.

"Of course," he said. "This has been a confusing time for you. But I wouldn't wait too long. I fear the window of opportunity for your Golden Gate may not be open as long as you assume."

"I think the idea is safe as long as I have the blockchain architecture."

"I'm not talking about your blockchain. It is probably secure. As fast as today's supercomputers are, it would take them years to break your codes. But they might be child's play for quantum computers. And what, perhaps they are a decade away?"

I looked at Marat.

"He went to Wharton," the old man shrugged. "I guess the money was well-spent."

"I didn't learn about this in school," Arman explained. "But I've been reading up on blockchains and cryptocurrencies."

"Ok," I said. "I'll bite. What the hell is a quantum computer?"

"I think I'll let Dr. Annalise explain," Arman said.

We all looked at her.

"Quantum theory holds that subatomic particles can exist in more than one state at any time. Regular computers use bits of numbers, 1 and 0, to calculate. The supercomputers we all know about can crunch billions of these bits a second. Quantum computers also use the 1 and 0 system. But their 1s and 0s exist in constantly changing states simultaneously and are called 'qubits'. They can store much more information. Each qubit increases computing power exponentially. If properly harnessed, quantum computers might be able to do trillions of calculations a second. It's been estimated that a single quantum computer with 100 qubits would be more powerful than all the existing supercomputers on Earth."

"And that's bad for blockchains?" I asked.

"Theoretically. Bitcoin miners are just computers that add new blocks of data to a chain. The algorithms are huge and so it still takes a modern computer about 10 minutes to create, or mine, a single new block. Remember what I told you in the Murray about hashes. Each new block contains a hash of the preceding block in the chain, which is why blockchains are practically invulnerable to hacking by current computers."

"What is the Murray?" Arman asked.

"Oh, it's just a restaurant I took Alton to."

"Still got the way with the ladies, I see, Alton," Arman said. "What else did you talk about? Nuclear physics?"

"Anyway," Anna continued, "a quantum computer might be able to crack a blockchain in seconds. Theoretically. And quantum computers will be most useful in biology, gene-splicing, astrophysics and the like."

"Eventually, however," Arman said. "The crooks will use them. Take it from an expert in that arena. But I agree it is years away. And perhaps by then you will have thought of a safeguard, Anna. Still, it is something to consider."

There was a knock on the door. Kalugin got up again. More waiters appeared. Some cleared our soup course, while others laid out platters of broiled grouper, red snapper, side dishes, or poured more wine.

As we passed platters around, I looked at Arman. We smiled at each other. Anna was in good hands. Arman was nothing if not a quick study. I suspected that the Rahms would have no trouble partnering with Anna on Golden Gate. Mel the accountant and his acolytes would undoubtedly have plenty to do when they got out of Okahumpka Correctional.

I also suspected that Annalise Purna was on her

way to becoming a very rich woman. And from the way she was now looking at Arman, he was going to be the next target of her affections.

We all tucked into our delicious food, and the two of them continued their high-tech conversation. I looked down at my snapper, which still had its head on and looked completely disinterested. I couldn't help thinking that the human race, with its cryptocurrencies and quantum computers, had come a long way since our aquatic ancestors had crawled up on dry land half a billion years ago.

Then, maybe not. As far as I knew, no fish ever threw someone from a balcony.

After dinner we dropped Anna back at the Kiernans. She had to pack for her trip back to San Francisco. The Rahms owned their own home in another section of town. It was two stories, had a circular driveway, fronted a big lake and was decidedly not modest. I counted four golf carts.

CHAPTER 38 - HOMECOMING

The next morning, we breakfasted at the Kiernans. The soda bread was good, but wasn't up to New York standards. Probably the local water. Then, we drove to Orlando.

Anna and I parted at the airport terminal where she would catch a flight to the West Coast. Her goodbye kiss lacked the fervor of the day before, which I attributed to her subtle shift in affection toward Arman. That was fine with me, and I know it made Maks happy.

"I'll be out to see you next week," Arman told Anna.

"I can't wait," she replied.

I wondered if I should warn Arman what he was getting into.

When we got back in the Bentley he said, "What are you smiling about, Alton?"

"Nothing."

They dropped me at my terminal, and I caught a flight into Newark.

***

I'd called Alice. She wanted to cut her teaching classes at Barnard and pick me up. I was anxious to see her, of course. But also dreaded explaining everything. Other than a few hurried earlier phone calls to tell her I wasn't making much progress, she was in the dark about the most recent events, which included such highlights as the car bomb, basement torture, shootings and international financial conspiracies.

Confirming her suspicions about Kevin Allender's death would not be a walk in the park, either.

Then, there was how I looked. Physically, I felt much better. My limp was less pronounced. But my face still had a variety of colors, not to mention stitches. The tried-and-true "I fell down a flight of stairs" explanation wouldn't work with Alice, and I knew she'd feel guilty about almost getting me killed, no matter how many times I insisted she was worth it.

So, I told her I had to go to the office and could pick her up at the ferry that afternoon. I couldn't help but think of what happened the last time I planned to do that.

***

When Alice got in the car, she leaned over to kiss me. Her eyes widened.

"What happened to your face?"

"Maks said it is an improvement. But I'll get to that later. But first I want to tell you about Kevin."

So, I did. By the time we got to my house, she was crying. Just a bit.

"I'm not crying because I still love Kevin," she said. "I love you. But it's just so sad. I don't understand. What did he ever do to anyone?"

"Let's go inside. I'll pour us a couple of drinks and explain everything."

"Oh, God. You're limping, too," Alice said as we walked to the door. "I'm so sorry."

She started crying again. I kissed her. Hard.

"Cut it out. You've heard the worst part. Some of the stuff I have to tell you is pretty funny, when you think about it."

Inside, as I made our martinis, Alice said, "Where is Gunner?"

"I left him with the Rahm people for one more day. I only want you to slobber over me tonight."

That got a small laugh. And as I explained things some more, she managed a few wry smiles. But then she turned serious again.

"Poor Kevin. He was always an idealist, which is what attracted him to me in the first place. But he was also so conflicted. Being smart with numbers, he had no problem getting a job on Wall Street. He convinced himself, and me, I guess, that was what he wanted to do. He was so convincing that we drifted apart."

I wanted to say that I was glad they had, but I kept my mouth shut.

"I've told you that he wanted us to move from Greenwich Village to Long Island and start a family. But by then it made no sense, and we both knew it. So, we divorced. But Rosemary told me a while ago that while Kevin made good money and was well respected, he wasn't happy with the way his life had turned out. I guess he was rebelling against the things he saw on Wall Street. So, I'm not surprised he'd try to lend his financial acumen to a project that would help society."

"He did more than lend, Alice," I said. "Anna said Golden Gate was his idea to begin with."

"And he was killed by someone who was no more than a common criminal," Alice said. "A bank robber, when you come right down to it, even if it was his own bank. Not even interested in Kevin's brilliance, or cryptocurrencies. Just in using him and his idea to steal real money. It's all so tawdry."

I took Alice's hand.

"If it matters, honey, Anna has promised to name the bitcoin they mine the 'Allender' in his honor. And to make sure that his sister and her kids are well taken care of, with real money. Arman has promised, as well."

"It matters."

Alice sighed deeply.

"Sometimes, life really sucks, Alton."

"Not all the time, I hope."

She leaned over to me, took my head in her hands and gave me a long kiss. There is something about kissing a woman you love that is hard to explain. It's just different. Visceral.

Then Alice looked deeply in my eyes.

"Alton, you have been wonderful. Not many men would have taken such an interest in what happened to their lover's ex-husband."

"Aw, shucks, little lady. You're embarrassing me."

Her gaze deepened.

"Then, this should really embarrass you. I think we should get married."

I laughed. Alice was so startled she sat back.

"What's so goddamn funny?"

"Hold that thought," I said, and went into the kitchen and opened the fridge.

"Alton?"

Alice sounded exasperated. She probably thought I was getting a snack.

When I returned, I had the bottle of Veuve Cliquot Brut and two champagne flutes in one hand.

And the little blue box in the other.

I knelt in front of her.

And didn't even feel the stitches I pulled in my thigh.

THE END

THE ALTON RHODE MYSTERY SERIES BEGAN WITH *CAPRIATI'S BLOOD.* HERE IS AN EXCERPT:

PROLOGUE

"They look smaller than the last bunch."

"You'll get more in the box," the elderly woman working the counter said. "Same price. You can't beat it."

"They taste the same?"

"If anything, they are sweeter." She pointed to a stand a few feet away. "We have some free samples cut up over there. Try them."

The man looked over at the table and saw that some flies hadn't needed an invitation.

"I'll take your word for it." His mother probably wouldn't know the difference. At least that was what he'd been told. The information had eased his conscience. Why risk a visit to someone who wouldn't even recognize her own son? But perhaps the occasional – and anonymous – gifts would soon be unnecessary. But just the thought of what he was going to do sent rivulets of sweat down the man's sides. "What do I owe you?"

"It comes to $34.95, shipping included east of the Mississippi."

Prices were going up on everything.

"Where's it going?"

The customer recited the address. Three times. Like everyone else in the goddamn town, the clerk was a few years past her expiration date. That was one reason he was about to take the biggest risk of his life.

"Want to include a card?"

"No."

"What's the return address?"

"If it doesn't get there," he said, smiling. "I don't want them back."

"I know, but we can apply a refund to your account."

"I don't have an account."

"It would be credited to your card. We take them all. American Express, MasterCard, Visa, Discover. Debit cards, too."

"I'm paying cash, don't worry about it."

"Well, if you give us your address, phone number and email, we can contact you."

He wanted to throttle the old crone. But long ago, for safety's sake, the man learned not to make a scene.

"No, thanks."

"We send out emails about our specials. People love them."

He took a deep breath and forced another smile. Then he pulled out his wallet and handed the woman $40.

"Just send the box. Keep the change."

***

It took the man an hour and a half to drive to Fort Lauderdale and settle in at the rundown motel off

Dixie Highway straight out of the 1980's and run by a couple of Russians, which he thought was ironic considering what he was about to do. He registered using one of the many phony I.D.'s he'd collected over the years. They'd wanted a credit card at the desk "for incidentals," which from the look of the place might include pest control, but the extra hundred bucks he gave them along with the room charge he prepaid shut the Russkies up. They assumed he just wanted to get laid and didn't want to leave a paper trail. They were half right.

The call he planned to make on the room phone wasn't going to cost a hundred bucks. It would be short, sweet and to the point. A previous call, made a few days earlier from a similar dump in Sarasota, had insured that the lawyer would be in at 4 P.M. to take his call. The lawyer's secretary was a dim bulb but the mention that he had important information about the lawyer's main client finally sealed the deal.

The man looked at his watch. An hour to go. There was a bar across the street from the motel. He walked across and had three stiff bourbons. The last one barely managed to stop the tremor in his hand. One of the rummies sitting on a nearby stool smiled in commiseration. He pegs me as an alky like him, the man thought. He doesn't know I'm just scared shitless.

***

"It's that call you've been expecting, Mr. Rosenberg."

Samuel Rosenberg's secretary stood in the doorway to his office and could have announced the arrival of the Messiah with less fanfare. She was all of 22 and proof to him that the New York City public education system had gone into the toilet. He had tried to get her to use his first name and the phone intercom, with no luck on either.

Rosenberg sighed. She had only recently mastered the basic legal forms he rarely produced. His previous secretary was canned for running her mouth in the wrong places and the lawyer decided that if he had to choose between stupid and indiscreet, stupid was the way to go.

"Thank you, Francine," he said. "That's a fetching outfit you are wearing today."

She smiled and twirled away. Her clothes were still terrible, he knew, but at least they now covered her midriff. That was one battle won.

"This is Samuel Rosenberg," he said into the phone. He looked at the calendar on his desk for the name. "What can I do for you, er, Mr. Wagner?" He put his feet up on his desk and rocked back in his chair. "You mentioned something about one of my clients. I have many. Can you be more specific."

"Quit dicking around, counselor. You don't want me to be specific. We both know who we're talking about. I want you to be an intermediary between us. I have a proposal, a trade."

"I'm listening."

"I know who killed Fred Jarvis."

Rosenberg's feet came off the desk as he sat up. Like every attorney on Staten Island, he remembered the unsolved killing. Jarvis was a piece of crap, a crook, but a lawyer nonetheless. If crooked lawyers became targets on Staten Island, who was safe?

"If it wasn't you," Rosenberg said coldly, "then I suggest you contact the police. If you need representation, I can suggest someone. What does this have to do with my client?"

"Your client was with me. He saw everything, too."

Jesus H. Christ. He reached for a pad and noted the time, just because he felt he had to do something. He looked at the caller I.D. It said "Unknown Number."

"I thought that might get your attention. I guess he forgot to mention it. We were young, and just along for the ride, so to speak. Even so, we might have been implicated as accessories. Not that we were inclined to say anything back then. We were all just one happy family. But things have changed. I read the papers. He's got a shitpot of reasons why he'd want the murder solved now, capische? He would probably love to blow the whistle, but can't, not without corroboration. So, here's the deal."

After the man finished speaking, Rosenberg said, "I'll see what I can do."

"It won't be easy, pal, there is a slight problem."

"What's that?"

"Your client wants to kill me."

A half hour later Rosenberg pulled into the Crooke's Point Marina in Great Kills Harbor. Not for the first time he reflected that, considering who owned many of the boats docked there, the "e" could have been dropped from the marina's name.

Nando Carlucci was standing on the bridge of a Grady White whose engine was just then rumbling to life. Rosenberg climbed aboard clumsily. He didn't like boats, or fishing. But it was hard to bug a boat, especially when his client belonged to a boat club that allowed him the use of dozens of crafts of varying sizes on short notice. At least the Grady White was big enough to have an interior cabin. It really was cold. Ten minutes later he and Carlucci, the grossly overweight head of Staten Island's last remaining Italian crime family, were cruising a half mile offshore, far from any possible listening devices aimed their way. Yes, thank God for the Grady, Rosenbrg thought. Nando in anything smaller was an invitation to capsize.

"So, what the fuck is so urgent?"

The lawyer told him. Carlucci stared at him for a full minute.

"I can't believe the balls on the guy. After what he did to me. He's right, I'll kill him. What did he call himself?"

"Said his name was Wagner."

"Son of a bitch."

When Carlucci calmed down, he said, "What does he want?"

Rosenberg braced himself for another tirade.

"One million dollars and a head start after the trial."

Carlucci erupted again, flinging charts and ashtrays around the cabin. When he stopped, he said, "What do you think? Can you swing the deal?"

"I think so. It would be a feather in the D.A.'s cap. Can you swing the million?"

"Yeah, but tell him some of it has to be in jewelry, mostly diamonds."

Rosenberg didn't want to know where the jewelry was coming from. There had been a rash of burglaries in some of the borough's most upscale neighborhoods over the past few months. The cops were stumped, since some of the homes had state-of-the-art alarm systems. But the burglars vanished before the response cars arrived on the scene.

***

Wary at first, the D.A. and his assistants had grown more interested and animated as Carlucci and his lawyer outlined his plan in more detail during several secret meetings.

"We insist on full immunity for Mr. Carlucci," Rosenberg said, "as well as for the corroborating witness."

That had been the sticking point during the weeks of negotiations. The D.A. and his subordinates loathed

Nando Carlucci. The idea of letting the fat mobster off the hook for a murder was repugnant to them.

"But you still won't tell us who this alleged witness is," one of the A.D.A's said.

"You don't have to know that now," Rosenberg said. "You have nothing to lose. We're the ones who have to produce. Mr. Carlucci wants to do his civic duty and clear his conscience, even though he was but an innocent bystander in the lamentable affair."

In the end, the D.A. went along with it.

"We'll get Carlucci eventually," he said after the meeting. "One big fish at a time."

As they drove away from the D.A.'s office, Rosenberg said, "I hope you know what you're doing, Nando. This is a big risk. Opens up a can of worms. He'd better produce."

"Don't you worry, counselor. He'll produce. He wants it bad."

"It's not just you, Nando. I've got my reputation to think of. My name will be anathema with the D.A. if we stiff him on this."

Carlucci looked at his lawyer with ill-concealed contempt.

"Your fuckin' name is an enema. You got no reputation to protect. Just do your job and wrap up the immunity thing tighter than a virgin's pussy. I don't have to remind you what happened to the last lawyer that fucked with my family, do I? That's how we got here, ain't it?"

***

CHAPTER 1 – THE RED LANTERN

Two Months Later

The workmen wheeled the last of the potted plant life into my office on hand dollies.

"You sure you don't want us to put some out in the reception area, Mr. Rhode?"

"I haven't finished painting it and the carpet is coming next week," I said. "I'd only have to move them all."

He shrugged and handed me an envelope.

"Miss Robart wrote down some instructions on how to care for them. She said if you have any questions, just call."

I'm not a plant guy. I'd keep the hardiest. The best shot at survival for the rest was my plan to donate them to other offices in the building. I called Nancy Robart at the Staten Island Botanical Garden to thank her for the foliage. She was the Executive Director and had donated the plants to give my new digs "some much needed class." She was at a luncheon, so I left the thank you on her voice mail.

Lunch sounded good to me. I opened a drawer in my desk, dropped Nancy's instructions in it and pulled out the holster containing my .38 Taurus Special. A lot of people in my line of work don't carry guns. Most of them have never been shot at, in war or peace. I have, in both, and like the comforting feel of iron on my hip.

Besides, with all the hoops you have to jump through to get a permit in New York City (if you fill out the paperwork wrong they send you to Guantanamo), it seems silly not to carry. The Taurus revolver has only five chambers in its cylinder, to keep the weight down. But the bullets are big. The gun is meant for close-in work. Presumably if you need more than five shots a sixth won't matter.

I clipped the holster on my belt and shrugged into the brown corduroy jacket that was draped on the back of my chair. The jacket felt a little tight around the shoulders. I wasn't back to my old weight but my rehab, which included lifting iron, was redistributing muscle. I'd have to get my clothes altered soon. Or, assuming I got some clients, buy some new threads. But the jacket still fell nicely, even if it didn't quite cover the paint smudges on my jeans, and there was no gun bulge.

I walked down the stairs to the building lobby. The docs at the V.A. hospital said it would help strengthen my leg and it seemed to be working. The limp was barely noticeable. I stopped at the security station by the elevators and told the guard that I'd left my office unlocked because the cable company was scheduled to install my high-speed Internet and phone system sometime in the afternoon.

"You're the private eye on eight," she said. "Rhode." Her name tag said "H. Jones" and she was sturdily stout without being fat. Her skin color was only slightly darker than her tan uniform. "What time they give you?"

"Sometime between 1 PM and the next ice age," I said.

"I hear you." She wrote something in a large cloth-bound ledger, the kind that used to sit on hotel check-in counters and private eyes were able to read upside down in noir movies. I never could read upside down, so the move to hotel computers made no difference to me. "You coming back?"

"Yeah. Just running out to pick up some lunch."

"Where you headed?"

"Red Lantern, in Rosebank. You know it?"

"Oh, man. Best eggplant hero in the borough."

"Can I bring one back for you?"

"Sure."

She bent to get her purse.

"Forget it. My treat. What's the 'H' stand for?"

"Habika. It means 'sweetheart,' in some African language I have no clue about. My folks had just seen *Roots* when I was born. Coulda been worse, I guess."

"Alton," I said, extending my hand.

"Like I said, it coulda been worse," she said. "You can call me 'Abby'. Everyone else does. Abby Jones."

"Why not sweetheart, or sweetie?"

"Cause then I hit you upside your head. Listen, my brother works at the cable company. I'll give him a call to make sure they don't forget about you."

A Rhode rule: It never hurts to buy an eggplant hero for a security guard.

There was a bank branch in the lobby. It had an ATM but the daily limit was $400 and I had a bar tab to square. I was working off the cash from a dwindling home equity line of credit inexplicably approved by the same bank. I wondered if I could be nailed for trading on inside information if I shorted its stock because it lent me the money.

The branch manager came out of his cubbyhole to shake my hand, smiling effusively. He led me over to a cute little redhead teller who thanked me before, during and after the transaction. If I'd wanted a toaster, she would have gone home and taken one from her own kitchen. The banks had a lot of PR ground to make up.

I now had a grand in my pocket. Flush and hungry; a combination that always works for me. I planned to walk the mile or so along Bay Street to the Red Lantern. But it was drizzling, with the imminent promise of something heavier. With a corduroy jacket I'd weigh as much as Donald Trump's hairdo by the time I arrived. I don't use an umbrella unless animals are lining up two-by-two on the ark ramp.

My three-year old light blue Chevy Malibu is distinguished only by several round indentations on its trunk and rear panels. I'd bought it at Honest Al Lambert's Used Car Lot in Tottenville. Al had acquired six almost-pristine Malibus at auction from a rental fleet, but hadn't counted on the car carrier transporting them from Denver running into a vicious hail storm in Indiana. The vehicles on top had their windshields smashed and their bodywork turned into the far side of the moon. Undaunted, Al tried to sell me one of those. But even the dimmest suspect might notice being followed by a car with more dimples than a golf ball. So, I opted for one of the Malibus on the carrier's first level, which sustained little damage but were still heavily discounted. It looked like every third car on the road. Still, I made a few modifications, including a passenger-side ejector seat activated by a red button hidden in the gear shift. I didn't actually do that.

At the Red Lantern all the parking spots, including those next to fire hydrants, bus stops and "No Parking" signs, were filled with cars that had official stickers or emblems: police, fire, sanitation, court officers, judges, Borough Hall, Coast Guard. Coast Guard? The NFL season was in full swing. It was Friday and the regular lunchtime crowd was inflated by dozens of people dropping off betting slips for Sunday's games in the bar's huge football pool. My glove compartment was full of phony decals and emblems that I would have used in an illegal spot if one was available, but I couldn't chance double parking and blocking in some Supreme Court judge. I settled for a spot two blocks away.

This section of Rosebank, once almost exclusively Italian, with a sprinkling of Jewish delis and bakeries, now had businesses run by more recent immigrants. I passed a Korean nail salon flanked by an Indian restaurant and a Pakistani convenience store. Across the street was something called the Somali-American Social Club, where a tall man in a white dashiki stood outside smoking. Probably didn't want to light up inside near the explosives. Two doors down, Gottleib's Bakery, a local institution for 80 years, still held the fort. If World War III broke out, I was pretty certain it would start here.

Inside the Red, patrons were two-deep at the rail keeping three bartenders hopping. All the tables in the front and back rooms were occupied and I pushed my way to the bar. The front room had dimpled tin ceilings that tended to amplify and redirect noise. In fact, because of an acoustic anomaly, something said at one end of the bar might be heard clearly at the other end. Of course, most conversations were lost in the mix of babble, but people still tended to be discreet. If you wanted to ask for a quick blow job in the car, or you were a city councilman asking five large in cash from a contractor who needed a zoning variance, you might as well put it on cable. The half-oval bar ran the length of the front room and had a dark green leather border matched by the upholstery of high-back swivel stools. A large silver trophy depicting a crouching man with his hand swept back occupied a place of honor next to the register. Its nameplate read "R. Kane." Underneath that, "1973 Tri-State Handball Championships." A third line said "Second Place."

Roscoe Kane, 60 pounds past his handball prime, lumbered over. I reached in my pocket, counted off $500 and put it on the bar.

"Take me off the books."

"Business picking up?"

"I'm being optimistic."

Reaching behind the register, Roscoe pulled out a beat-up marble notebook of the type your mother bought for your first day of school. He laid it on the bar, flipped some pages, picked up a pencil and crossed something out. He took $420 from the pile and put it in the cash drawer. At the same time, he reached down into a cooler, lifted out a bottle of Sam Adams Light, twisted off the cap with one hand and slid it down to me. Ex-handball champs don't lack for manual dexterity. He put the notebook away. I knew that dozens, maybe hundreds, of similar notebooks had served the same purpose since the Red Lantern, one of the oldest taverns in the city, opened its doors back when the Kings Rifles garrisoned Staten Island.

Roscoe put some bar nuts in front of me and said, "Glass? Lunch?"

"No, and yes," I said through a mouthful of nuts. "Two eggplant heroes to go."

I took a long draw on my beer. It was ice cold. Not too many people drank Sam Adams in the Red, let alone Sam Adams Light, but Roscoe kept in a stash for me. It was the only light beer I'd ever had that didn't taste light.

I said, "Is it true that the Algonquins ran a tab in here?"

"Never. Bastards stiffed us."

"Yeah," one of the regulars at the bar snorted, "and this place hasn't bought back a drink since."

As I sipped my beer, I turned to scan the opposite wall, which was covered floor to ceiling with tally sheets for the 1,400 people in the football pool. The alphabetically-listed entrants were a democratic cross section of the populace, including just about every elected and appointed official, several judges, a smattering of assistant district attorneys, college professors, scores of cops and half the hoods in the borough. The sheets were taken down after the Monday night games and updated by the three elderly Italian ladies who also ran the kitchen. No one questioned their cooking or their accuracy.

I felt a blast of chilly air. The bar's cheerful hubbub eased a bit and one of the other bartenders said "shit" under his breath. I turned as Arman Rahm and a fire hydrant entered the bar. The fire hydrant's name was Maks Kalugin and had more bullet holes in him than Emperor Maximilian.

END OF EXCERPT

THE JAKE SCARNE THRILLERS

SOUND OF BLOOD

MADMAN'S THIRST

KILLERFEST

THE VIRON CONSPIRACY

PEDESTAL

FACETS

CHANCE

THE ALTON RHODE MYSTERIES

CAPRIATI'S BLOOD

LAURA LEE

SIREN'S TEARS

SISTER

GUNNER

THE ELSON LEGACY

TURTLE DOVE

SHADOW OF THE BLACK WOMB

GOLDEN GATE

THE COLE SUDDEN C.I.A. ACTION THRILLERS

SUDDEN KILL

THE HADRON ESCAPE

THAWED

CHILDREN'S BOOKS

THE PURLOINED PONIES

ABOUT THE AUTHOR

Lawrence De Maria began his career as a general interest reporter (winning an Associated Press award for his crime reporting) and eventually became a Pulitzer-nominated senior editor and financial writer *The New York Times*, where he wrote hundreds of stories and features, often on Page 1. After he left the *Times*, De Maria became an Executive Director at *Forbes*.

Following a stint in corporate America – during which he helped uncover the $7 billion Allen Stanford Ponzi scheme and was widely quoted in the national media – he returned to journalism as Managing Editor of the *Naples Sun Times*, a Florida weekly, until its sale to the Scripps chain in 2007. Since then, he has been a full-time fiction writer.

De Maria is on the board of directors of the Washington Independent Review of Books, where, when he's not killing people in his novels, he writes features, reviews and a column.

Thank You for Reading This Book!

For a small press such as St. Austin's, getting exposure in the market place in competition with the publishing giants is one of the key challenges. But it is also one where you, as a reader, can help enormously by spreading the word.

So, if you have enjoyed this book, please help promote the author, Lawrence De Maria, and St. Austin's Press.

There's a wide range of ways you can do so:

- *Recommend the book to your friends*
- *Post a review on Amazon or other book websites*
- *Review it on your blog*
- *Tweet about it and provide a link to www.lawrencedemaria.com*
- *Post links to that website on your Facebook, LinkedIn or other social media pages*
- *Pin the website, or individual books, at Pinterest*
- *Anything else that you think of!*

Many thanks for your help – it's much appreciated.